John Thomas Smi

The Cries of London

outlook

John Thomas Smith

The Cries of London

1st Edition | ISBN: 978-3-75242-695-3

Place of Publication: Frankfurt am Main, Germany

Year of Publication: 2020

Outlook Verlag GmbH, Germany.

Reproduction of the original.

THE CRIES OF LONDON:

BY

JOHN THOMAS SMITH,

INTRODUCTION.

There are few subjects, perhaps, so eagerly attended to by the young as those related by their venerable parents when assembled round the fire-side, but more particularly descriptions of the customs and habits of ancient times. Now as the Cries of London are sometimes the topic of conversation, the author of the present work is not without the hope of finding, amongst the more aged as well as juvenile readers, many to whom it may prove acceptable, inasmuch as it not only exhibits several Itinerant Traders and other persons of various callings of the present day, but some of those of former times, collected from engravings executed in the reigns of James I., Charles I. and during the Usurpation of Oliver Cromwell, and which, on account of their extreme rarity, are seldom to be seen but in the most curious and expensive Collections.

In the perusal of this volume the collector of English Costume, as well as the Biographer, may find something to his purpose, particularly in the old dresses, as it was the custom for our forefathers to wear habits peculiar to their station, and not, as in the present times, when a linen-draper's apprentice, or a gentleman's butler, may, in the boxes of the theatre, by means of his dress, and previously to uttering a word, be mistaken for the man of fashion.

Of all the itinerant callings the Watchman, the Water Carrier, the Vender of Milk, the Town Crier, and the Pedlar, are most probably of the highest antiquity.

When the Suburbs of London were infested with wolves and other depredators, and the country at large in a perpetual state of warfare, it was found expedient for the inhabitants to protect themselves, and for that purpose they surrounded their city by a wall, and according to the most ancient custom erected barbicans or watch-towers at various distances, commanding a view of the country, so that those on guard might see the approach of an enemy. This is an extremely ancient custom, as we find in the Second Book of Kings, chapter ix. verse 17, "And there stood a watchman on the Tower in Jezreel."

With respect to water, it is natural to suppose that before conduits were established in London, the inhabitants procured it from the River Thames, and that infirm people, and the more opulent citizens, compensated others for the

2

trouble of bringing it.

This must have also been the practice as to milk, in consequence of the farm-houses always being situated in the suburbs for the purpose of grazing the cattle. Stowe, the historian, has informed us that in his boyish days he had his three quarts of milk hot from the cow for his halfpenny.

The Water Carrier will be described and delineated in the course of this work.

As the city increased in population, a Town Crier became expedient, so that an article to be sold, or any thing lost, might be in the shortest possible time made known to the inhabitants of the remotest dwelling. Shakspeare has marked the character of a Crier of his time in Hamlet, Act iii. scene 2, "But if you mouth it, as many of our players do, I had as lieve the Town-crier spoke my lines." Lazarello de Tormes, in the very entertaining history of his life, describes his having been a Crier at Madrid, and that by blowing a horn he announced the sale of some wine.

Sometimes the criers of country towns afford instances of the grossest flattery and ignorance. We have an instance in the Crier of Cowbridge, Glamorganshire, who, after announcing the loss of an "all black cow, with a white face and a white tail," concluded with the usual exclamation of "God save the King and the Lord of the Manor!" adding, "and Master Billy!" well knowing that the Lord of the Manor or his Lady would remember him for recollecting their infant son.

It may be inferred from an ancient stained glass picture of a pedlar with his pack at his back, still to be seen in a South-east window of Lambeth Church, [4] a representation of which has been given by the author in a work entitled, "Antiquities of London," that itinerant trades must have been of long standing.

It appears from the celebrated Comedy of Ignoramus, by George Ruggle, performed before King James the First on March the 8th, 1614, of which there is an English translation by Robert Codrington, published 1662, that books were at that period daily cried in the streets.

In the third scene of the second act, *Cupes* the itinerant Bibliopole exclaims,

Libelli, belli, belli; lepidi, novi libelli; belli, belli, libelli!

Trico. Heus, libelli belli.

Cupes. O Trico, mox tibi operam do. Ita vivam, ut pessimi sunt libelli.

In the time of Charles II. ballad singers and *sellers of small books* were required to be licensed. John Clarke, bookseller, rented the licensing of all ballad-singers of Charles Killigrew, Esq. master of the revels, for five years, which term expired in 1682. "These, therefore, are to give notice (saith the latter gentleman in the London Gazette) to all ballad-singers, that they take out licenses at the office of the Revels at Whitehall, for singing and selling of ballads and small books, according to an antient custom. And all persons concerned are hereby desired to take notice of, and to suppress, all mountebanks, rope-dancers, prize-players, ballad-singers, and such as make shew of motions and strange sights, that have not a license in red and black letters, under the hand and seal of the said Charles Killigrew, Esq. Master of the Revels to his Majesty; and in particular, to suppress one Mr. Irish, Mr. Thomas Varney, and Thomas Yeats, mountebank, who have no license, that they may be proceeded against according to law."

The Gazette of April 14, 1684, contains another order relative to these licenses: "All persons concerned are hereby desired to take notice of and suppress all mountebanks, rope-dancers, ballad-singers, &c. that have not a license from the Master of his Majesty's Revels (which, for this present year, are all printed with black letters, and the King's Arms in red) and particularly Samuel Rutherford and —— Irish, mountebanks, and William Bevel and Richard Olsworth; and all those that have licenses with red and black letters, are to come to the office to change them for licenses as they are now altered."

The origin of our early cries might be ascribed to the parent of invention. An industrious man finding perhaps his trade running slack, might have ventured abroad with his whole stock, and by making his case known, invited his neighbours to purchase; and this mode of vending commodities being adopted by others, probably established the custom of itinerant hawkers, to the great and truly serious detriment of those housekeepers who contributed to support their country by the payment of their taxes. An Act was passed in the reign of James the First, and is thus noticed in a work entitled, "Legal Provisions for the Poor, by S. C. of the Inner Temple, 1713." "All Pedlars, Petty-chapmen, Tinkers, and Glass-men, *per Statute* 21 *Jac.* 28, *abroad*, especially if they be unknown, or have not a sufficient testimonial, and though a man have a certain habitation, yet if he goes about from place to place selling small wares, he is punishable by the 39 Eliz."

Hawkers and Pedlars are obliged at this time, in consequence of an Act passed in the reign of King George the Third, to take out a license.

Originally the common necessaries of life were only sold in the *streets*, but we find as early as the reign of Elizabeth that cheese-cakes were to be had at the small *house* near the Serpentine River in Hyde Park. It is a moated building, and to this day known under the appellation of the "Queen's Cheese-cake House."[5] There were also other houses for the sale of cheese-cakes, and those at Hackney and Holloway were particularly famous. The landlord of the latter employed people to cry them about the streets of London; and within the memory of the father of the present writer an old man delivered his cry of "Holloway Cheese-cakes," in a tone so whining and slovenly, that most people thought he said "All my teeth ache." Indeed among persons who have been long accustomed to cry the articles they have for sale, it is often impossible to guess at what they say.

An instance occurs in an old woman who has for a length of time sold mutton dumplings in the neighbourhood of Gravel Lane. She may be followed for a whole evening, and all that can be conjectured from her utterance is "Hot mutton trumpery."

In another instance, none but those who have heard the man, would for a moment believe that his cry of "Do you want a brick or brick dust?" could have been possibly mistaken for "Do you want a lick on the head?"

An inhabitant of the Adelphi, when an invalid, was much annoyed by the peevish and lengthened cry of "Venny," proceeding every morning and evening from a muffin-man whenever he rang his bell.

Many of the old inhabitants of Cavendish Square must recollect the mournful manner in which a weather-beaten Hungerford fisherman cried his "Large silver Eels, live Eels." This man's tones were so melancholy to the ears of a lady in Harley Street that she allowed the fellow five shillings a week to discontinue his cry in that neighbourhood; and there is at the present time a slip-shod wretch who annoys Portland Place and its vicinity generally twice, and sometimes three times a day, with what may be strictly called the braying of an ass, and all his vociferation is to inform the public that he sells water-cresses, though he appears to call "Chick-weed." Another Stentorian bawler, and even a greater nuisance in the same neighbourhood, seems to his unfortunate hearers to deal in "Cats'-meat," though his real cry is "Cabbage-plants."

The witty author of a tract entitled, "An Examination of certain Abuses, Corruptions, and Enormities, in the City of Dublin," written in the year 1732, says, "I would advise all new comers to look out at their garret windows, and there see whether the thing that is cried be *Tripes* or *Flummery*, *Buttermilk* or *Cowheels*; for, as things are now managed, how is it possible for an honest countryman just arrived, to find out what is meant, for instance, by the following words, '*Muggs, Juggs, and Porringers, up in the Garret, and down in the Cellar?*' I say, how is it possible for a stranger to understand that this jargon is meant as an invitation to buy a farthing's worth of milk for his breakfast or supper?"

Captain Grose, in his very entertaining little work, entitled "An Olio," in which there are many interesting anecdotes, notices several perversions of this kind, particularly one of a woman who sold milk.

Farthing mutton pies were made and continued to be sold within the memory of persons now living at a house which was then called the "Farthing Pie House," in Marylebone Fields, before the New Road was made between Paddington and Islington, and which house remains in its original state at the end of Norton Street, New Road, bearing the sign of the Green Man.

Hand's Bun House at Chelsea was established about one hundred and twenty years since, and probably was the first of its kind. There was also a famous bun-house at the time of George the Second in the Spa Fields, near the New River Head, on the way to Islington, but this was long since pulled down to make way for the sheep-pens, the site of which is now covered with houses.

The first notice which the writer has been able to obtain of the hot apple-dumpling women is in Ned Ward's very entertaining work, entitled "The London Spy," first published in 1698. He there states that Pancakes and "Diddle, diddle dumplings O!" were then cried in Rosemary Lane and its vicinity, commonly called Rag Fair. The representation of a dumpling-woman, in the reign of Queen Anne, is given by Laroon in his Cries of London, published 1711.[6]

With respect to hot potatoes, they must have been considerably more modern, as there are persons now living who declare them to have been eaten with great caution, and very rarely admitted to the table. The potatoe is a native of Peru in South America; it has been introduced into England about a century and a half; the Irish seem to have been the first general cultivators of it in the western parts of Europe.

Rice milk, furmety, and barley-broth were in high request at the time of Hogarth, about 1740. Boitard, a French artist, who was in England at that time, has left us a most spirited representation of the follies of the day in his print entitled "Covent Garden Morning Frolic," in which the barley-broth woman is introduced. Without detracting from the merit of the immortal Hogarth, this print, which is extremely rare, exhibits as much humour as any of his wonderful productions. A copy of this engraving with an explanatory account of the portraits which it exhibits, will be given by the author in his Topographical History of Covent Garden, a work for which he has been collecting materials for upwards of thirty years.[7]

The use of saloop is of very recent date. It was brought into notice, and first sold in Fleet Street one hundred years ago, at the house now No. 102, where lines in its praise were painted upon a board and hung up in the first room from the street, a copy of which will precede a print representing a saloop stall, given in this work.

Formerly strong waters were publicly sold in the streets, but since the duty has been laid on spirits, and an Act passed to oblige persons to take out a license for dealing in liquors, the custom of hawking such commodities has been discontinued.

The town, from the vigilance of the Police, has fortunately got rid of a set of people called Duffers, who stood at the corners of streets, inviting the unsuspicious countryman to lay out his money in silk handkerchiefs or waistcoat pieces, which they assured him in a whisper to have been smuggled. A notorious fellow of this class, who had but one eye, took his stand regularly near the gin-shop at the corner of Hog Lane, Oxford Street. The mode adopted by such men to draw the ignorant higgler into a dark room, where he was generally fleeced, was by assuring him that no one could see them, and as for a glass of old Tom, he would pay for that himself, merely for the pleasure of shewing his goods.

Though this custom of accosting passengers at the corners of streets is very properly done away with, yet the tormenting importunities of the barking shopkeeper is still permitted, as all can witness as they pass through Monmouth Street, Rosemary Lane, Houndsditch, and Moorfields. The public were annoyed in this way so early as 1626, as appears from the following passage in "Greene's Ghost:" "There are another sort of Prentices, that when they see a gentlewoman or a countriman minded to buy any thing, they will fawne upon them, with cap in hand, with 'What lacke you, gentlewoman? what lacke you, countriman? see what you lacke.'"

I

//.,1,./,,,11,11

WATCHMAN, BELLMAN, and BILLMAN.

PLATES I. II. III.

IT has been observed in the Introduction, that of all the callings, that of the Watchman is perhaps of the highest antiquity; and as few writers can treat on any subject without a quotation from honest John Stowe, the following extract is inserted from that valuable and venerable author:

"Then had yee, besides the standing watches, all in bright harnesse, in every ward and streete of this citie and suburbs, a marching watch that passed thro' the principal streets thereof, to wit, from the Little Conduit by Paule's gate, thro' West Cheape, by the Stocks, thro' Cornehill, by Leadenhall to Aldgate, then backe downe Fen-church Street, by Grasse Church, about Grasse-church Conduit, and by Grasse Church Streete into Cornehill, and through it into Cheape again, and so broke up. The whole way ordered for this marching watch extended to 3200 taylors yards of assize. For the furniture thereof with lights there were appointed 700 cressets, 500 of them being found by the Companies, and the other 200 by the Chamber of London.[8] Besides the which lights, every Constable in London, in number more then 240, had his cresset; the charge of every cresset was in light two shillings and four pence, and every cresset had two men, one to beare or hold it, another to beare a bagge with light, and to serve it; so that the poore men pertaining to the cressets, taking wages, besides that every one had a strawne hat, with a badge painted, and his breakfast in the morning, amounted in number to almost 2000. The marching watch contained in number 2000 men, part of them being old souldiers, of skill to be captaines, lieutenants, serjeants, corporals, &c. Wiflers, drummers, and fifes, standard and ensigne bearers, sword-players, trumpeters on horsebacke, demilaunces on great horses, gunners with hand-guns, or halfe hakes, archers in coates of white fustian, signed on the breast and backe with the armes of the City, their bowes bent in their hands, with sheafes of arrowes by their sides, pikemen in bright corslets, burganets, &c. holbards, the like Billmen in Almaine rivets, and apernes of mayle, in great number."[9]

Mr. Douce observes, that these watches were "laid down 20 Henry VIII.;" and that "the Chronicles of Stow and Byddel assign the sweating sickness as a cause for discontinuing the watch."

"Anno 1416. Sir Henry Barton being maiar, ordained lanthorns and lights to be hang'd out on the winter evenings, betwixt Alhallows and Candlemas."

Mr. Warton, in his notes to Milton's Poems, observes, that anciently the Watchmen who cried the hours used the following or the like benedictions, which are to be found in a little poem called "The Bellman," inserted in Robert Herrick's Hesperides:

"From noise of scare-fires rest ye free,
From murder, Benedicite.
From all mischances, that may fright
Your pleasing slumbers in the night;
Mercie secure ye all, and keep
The goblin from ye while ye sleep." 1647.

The First Plate of the Watchman, introduced in this work, is copied from a rare woodcut sheet-print engraved at the time of James the First, consisting of twelve distinct figures of trades and callings, six men and six women. Under this Watchman the following verses are introduced, but they are evidently of a more modern date than that of the woodcut:

"Maids in your smocks, look to your locks,
    Your fire and candle light;
For well 'tis known, much mischief's done
    By both in dead of night.
Your locks and fire do not neglect,
And so you may good rest expect."

Under another Watchman, in the same set of figures, are the following lines, of the same type and orthography as the preceding:

"A light here, maids, hang out your light,
And see your horns be clear and bright,
That so your candle clear may shine,
Continuing from six till nine;
That honest men that walk along,
May see to pass safe without wrong."

There were not only Watchmen, but Bellmen and Billmen. These people were armed with a long bill in case of fire, so that they could, as the houses were mostly of timber, stop the progress of the flames by cutting away connections of fuel.

Of this description of men, the Second Plate, copied from a rare print prefixed to a work, entitled, "Villanies discovered by Lanthorne and Candle-light,"[10] by T. Deckar, or Dekker, 1616, is given as a specimen. The Bellman is stiled "The Childe of Darkness, a common Night-walker, a man that had no man to waite uppon him, but onely a dog, one that was a disordered person, and at midnight would beate at men's doores, bidding them (in meere mockerie) to

12

look to their candles when they themselves were in their dead sleeps, and albeit he was an officer, yet he was but of light carriage, being knowne by the name of the Bellman of London."

In Strype's edition of Stowe's London, 1756, (vol. ii. 489,) it is observed, "Add to this government of the nightly watches, there is belonging to each ward a Bellman, who, especially in the long nights, goeth thro' the streets and lanes, ringing a bell; and when his bell ceaseth, he salutes his masters and mistresses with some rhimes, suitable to the festivals and seasons of the year; and bids them look to their lights. The beginning of which custom seems to be in the reign of Queen Mary, in January 1556; and set up first in Cordwainer-street Ward, by Alderman Draper, Alderman of that ward; then and there, as I find in an old Journal, one began to go all night with a bell; and at every lane's end, and at the ward's end, gave warning of fire and candle, and to helpe the poor, and pray for the dead."

It appears from the Bellman's Epistle, prefixed to the London Bellman, published in 1640, that he came on at midnight, and remained ringing his bell till the rising up of the morning. He says, "I will wast out mine eies with my candles, and watch from midnight till the rising up of the morning: my bell shall ever be ringing, and that faithfull servant of mine (the dog that follows me) be ever biting."

Leases of houses, and household furniture stuff, were sold in 1564 by an out-cryer and bellman for the day, who retained one farthing in the shilling for his pains.

The friendly Mr. George Dyer, late a printseller of Compton-street, presented to the writer a curious sheet print containing twelve Trades and Callings, published by Overton, without date, but evidently of the time of Charles the Second, from which engraving the Third Plate of a Watchman was copied.

WATER-CARRIER.

PLATE IV.

THE Conduits of London and its environs, which were established at an early period, supplied the metropolis with water until Sir Hugh Middleton brought the New River from Amwell to London, and then the Conduits gradually fell into disuse, as the New River water was by degrees laid on in pipes to the principal buildings in the City, and, in the course of time, let into private houses.

When the above Conduits supplied the inhabitants, they either carried their vessels, or sent their servants for the water as they wanted it; but we may suppose that at an early period there were a number of men who for a fixed sum carried the water to the adjoining houses. The first delineation the writer has been able to discover of a Water-carrier, is in Hoefnagle's print of Nonsuch, published in the reign of Queen Elizabeth.

The next is in the centre of that truly-curious and more rare sheet wood-cut, entitled, "Tittle-Tattle," which from the dresses of the figures must have been engraved either in the latter part of the reign of Queen Elizabeth, or the beginning of that of James the First. In this wood-cut the maid servants are at a Conduit, where they hold their tittle-tattle, while the Water-carriers are busily engaged in filling their buckets and conveying them on their shoulders to the places of destination.

The figure of a Water-carrier, introduced in the Fourth Plate, is copied from one of a curious and rare set of cries and callings of London, published by Overton, at the White Horse without Newgate. The figure retains the dress of Henry the Eighth's time; his cap is similar to that usually worn by Sir Thomas More, and also to that given in the portrait of Albert Durer, engraved by Francis Stock. It appears by this print, that the tankard was borne upon the shoulder, and, to keep the carrier dry, two towels were fastened over him, one to fall before him, the other to cover his back. His pouch, in which we are to conclude he carried his money, has been thus noticed in a very curious and rare tract, entitled, *"Green's Ghost*, with the merry Conceits of Doctor Pinchbacke,"* published 1626: "To have some store of crownes in his purse, coacht in a faire trunke flop, like a boulting hutch."

Ben Jonson, in his admirable comedy of "Every Man in his Humour," first performed in 1598, has made Cob the water-carrier of the Old Jewry, at whose house Captain Bobadil lodges, a very leading and entertaining character. Speaking of himself before the Justice, he says, "I dwell, Sir, at the sign of the Water-tankard, hard by the Green Lattice; I have paid scot and lot there many time this eighteen years."

The first notice which the writer has been able to obtain of the introduction of the New River water into public buildings in London, he found in the Archives of Old Bethlem, in which it appears, that "on the 26th of February, 1626, Mr. Middleton conveyed water into Bethlem." This must have been, according to its date, the old Bethlem Hospital that stood in Bishopsgate-street, near St. Botolph's Church, on the site of the streets which are at this time under the denomination of Old Bethlem; as the building lately taken down in London Wall, Moorfields, was begun in April 1675, and finished in July 1676. It should seem therefore that this magnificent building, which had more the appearance of a palace than a place of confinement, most substantially built with a centre and two wings, extending in length to upwards of 700 feet, was only one year in building; a most extraordinary instance of manual application.

In 1698, when Cheapside Conduit was no longer used for its original purpose, it became the place of call for chimney-sweepers, who hung up their brooms and shovels against it, and there waited for hire.

It appears that even in 1711 the New River water was not generally let into houses; for in Laroon's Cries of London, which were published at that time, there is a man with two tubs suspended across his shoulders, according to the present mode of carrying milk, at the foot of which plate is engraved "Any New River Water, water here."[11]

CORPS-BEARER.

PLATE V.

OF all the calamities with which a great city is infested, there can be none so truly awful as that of a plague, when the street-doors of the houses that were visited with the dreadful pest were padlocked up, and only accessible to the surgeons and medical men, whose melancholy duty frequently exposed them even to death itself; and when the fronts of the houses were pasted over with large bills exhibiting red crosses, to denote that in such houses the pestilence was raging, and requesting the solitary passenger to pray that the Lord might have mercy upon those who were confined within. Of these bills there are many extant in the libraries of the curious, some of which have borders engraved on wood, printed in black, displaying figures of skeletons, bones, and coffins. They also contain various recipes for the cure of the distemper. The Lady Arundell, and other persons of distinction, published their methods for making what was then called plague-water, and which are to be found in many of the rare books on cookery of the time; but happily for London, it has not been visited by this affliction since 1665, a circumstance owing probably to the Great Fire in the succeeding year, which consumed so many old and deplorable buildings, then standing in narrow streets and places so confined that it was hardly possible to know where any pest would stop.

Every one who inspects Aggas's Plan of London, engraved in the reign of Elizabeth, as well as those published subsequently to the rebuilding of the City after the fire, must acknowledge the great improvements as to the houses, the widening of the streets, and the free admission of fresh air. It is to be hoped, and indeed we may conclude from the very great and daily improvements on that most excellent plan of widening streets, that this great City will never again witness such visitations.

When the plague was at its height, perhaps nothing could have been more silently or solemnly conducted than the removal of the dead to the various pits round London, that were opened for their reception; and it was the business of Corpse Bearers, such as the one exhibited in the Fifth Plate, to give directions to the Car-men, who went through the City with bells, which they rang, at the same time crying "Bring out your Dead." This melancholy description may be closed, by observing that many parts of London, particularly those leading to the Courts of Westminster, were so little trodden down, that the grass grew in the middle of the streets. Few persons would believe the truth of the following extract:

"A profligate wretch had taken up a new way of thieving (yet 'tis said too much practised in those times), of robbing the dead, notwithstanding the horror that is naturally concomitant. This trade he followed so long, till he furnished a warehouse with the spoils of the dead; and had gotten into his possession (some say) to the number of a thousand winding-sheets." See Memoirs of the Life and Death of Sir Edmundbury Godfrey, published 1682.

It is remarkable, and shows the great advantage of our River Thames, that during the Plague of 1665, according to a remark made by Lord Clarendon, not one house standing upon London Bridge was visited by the plague.

Although the subject of Funerals has been so often treated of by various authors, yet the following extracts will not, it is hoped, be deemed irrelevant by the reader. They may serve too as a contrast to the confusion and mingling of dust which must have taken place during the plague, in the burial of so many thousands in so short a space of time, and they may show likewise the vanity of human nature.

In "Chamberlain's Imitation of Holbein's Drawings," in his Majesty's collection, is the following passage alluding to the great care Lady Hobye took as to the arrangement of her funeral.

"Her fondness for those pompous soothings, which it was usual at that time for grief to accept at the hands of pride, scarcely died with her; for, a letter is extant from her to Sir William Dethick, Garter King of Arms, desiring to know 'what number of mourners were due to her calling; what number of waiting women, pages, and gentlemen ushers; of chief mourners, lords, and gentlemen; the manner of her hearse, of the heralds, and church?' &c. This remarkable epistle concludes thus: 'Good Mr. Garter, do it exactly, for I find forewarnings that bid me provide a pick-axe,' &c. The time of her death is not exactly known, but it is supposed to have been about 1596. She is buried at Bisham, with her first husband.[12] It was this Lady's daughter, Elizabeth Russell, that was said to have died with a pricked finger."

It was usual at funerals to use rosemary, even to the time of Hogarth, who has introduced it in a pewter plate on the coffin-lid of the funeral scene in his Harlot's Progress. Shakspeare notices it in Romeo and Juliet, "And stick your *rosemary* on this fair corse." "This plant," says Mr. Douce, in his "Illustrations of Shakspeare and Ancient Manners," page 216, vol. i. "was used in various ways at funerals. Being an evergreen, it was regarded as an emblem of the soul's immortality." Thus in Cartwright's "Ordinary," Act 5, scene 1:

> "————————If there be
> Any so kind as to accompany
> My body to the earth, let them not want
> For entertainment; pr'ythee see they have
> A *sprig of rosemary* dip'd in common water,
> To smell to as they walk along the streets."

In an obituary kept by Mr. Smith, secondary of one of the Compters, and preserved among the Sloanian MSS. in the British Museum, No. 886, is the following entry: "Jan. 2, 1671, Mr. Cornelius Bee, Bookseller in Little

Britain, died; buried Jan. 4, at Great St. Bartholomew's, without a sermon, without wine or wafers, only gloves and *rosemary*." And Mr. Gay, when describing Blowselinda's funeral, records that "Sprigg'd rosemary the lads and lasses bore."

Suicides were buried on the north side of the church, in ground purposely *unconsecrated*.

The custom of burial observed by that truly respectable class of the community denominated Friends, commonly called Quakers, may be deemed the most rational, as it is conducted with the utmost simplicity.

The corpse is kept the usual time; it is then put into a plain coffin uncovered. Afterwards it is placed in a plain hearse, also uncovered, and without feathers; the attendants accompanying the funeral in their family carriages, or hackney coaches. The corpse is then placed by the side of the grave where sometimes they offer a prayer, or deliver an exhortation, after which the coffin is lowered, the earth put over it, and thus the ceremony closes. Should the deceased have been a minister, then the corpse on the day of its interment is carried into the meeting house, and remains there in the midst of the congregation during their meditations.

The orthodox members of this society never wear any kind of mourning. Relatives are never designedly placed by each other, but are buried indiscriminately, as death may visit each member.

They begin at the left hand upper corner, placing them in rows till they have filled the ground to the lower right hand corner, after which they commence again as before. They make no distinction whatever between male and female, nor young and old, nor have they even so much as a coffin-plate.

The Jews bury their dead within four and twenty hours, adhering to the custom of the East, where the body would putrify beyond that time. The great burial-ground at Mile End was made at the sole expense of the famous Moses Hart, who, after losing an immense sum in the South Sea bubble, died worth 5000*l. per annum*. This munificent Jew also built the Dutch Synagogue in Duke's-place. The squib prints of the day designate Moses Hart by the introduction of the Knave of Hearts. The Knave of Clubs in the same plate was meant for the ancestor of the Gideon family. The Jews bury their poor by a collection made at the funerals of the better part of the community. Several boys go about to the mourners and other Jews assembled upon the occasion, with tin boxes padlocked up, at the top of which there is a small slit to admit of the contributions, and every Jew present, however humble his station, is eager to drop in his mite.

HACKNEY COACHMAN.

PLATE VI.

FROM the writer's extensive knowledge of prints, and his intimate acquaintance with the various collections in England, he has every reason to conclude that the original print of a Hackney Coachman, from which this Plate has been copied, is perhaps the only representation of the earliest character of that calling. The print from which it was taken is one of a Set published by Overton, at the sign of the White Horse without Newgate; and its similarity to the figures given by Francis Barlow in his Æsop's Fables, and particularly in a most curious sheet-print etched by that artist, exhibiting Charles the Second, the Duke of York, &c. viewing the Races on Dorset Ferry near Windsor, in 1687, sufficiently proves this Hackney Coachman to have been of the reign of that monarch.

The early Hackney Coachman did not sit upon the box as the present drivers do, but upon the horse, like a postilion; his whip is short for that purpose; his boots, which have large open broad tops, must have been much in his way, and exposed to the weight of the rain. His coat was not according to the fashion of the present drivers as to the numerous capes, which certainly are most rational appendages, as the shoulders never get wet; the front of the coat has not the advantage of the present folding one, as it is single breasted.

His hat was pretty broad, and so far he was screened from the weather. Another convincing proof that he rode as a postilion is, that his boots are spurred. In that truly curious print representing the very interesting Palace of Nonsuch, engraved by Hoefnagle, in the reign of Queen Elizabeth, the coachman who drives the royal carriage in which the Queen is seated, is placed on a low seat behind the horses, and has a long whip to command those he guides. How soon after Charles the Second's time the Hackney Coachmen rode on a box the writer has not been able to learn, but in all the prints of King William's time the Coachmen are represented upon the box, though by no means so high as at present; nor was it the fashion at the time of Queen Anne to be so elevated as to deprive the persons in the carriage of the pleasure of looking over their shoulders.

Brewer, in his "Beauties of Middlesex," observes in a note, that "It is familiarly said, that Hackney, on account of its numerous respectable inhabitants, was the first place near London provided with Coaches for hire, for the accommodation of families, and that thence arises the term Hackney

Coaches."

This appears quite futile; the word Hackney, as applied to a hireling, is traced to a remote British origin, and was certainly used in its present sense long before that village became conspicuous for wealth or population.

In 1637 the number of Hackney Coaches in London was confined to 50, in 1652 to 200, in 1654 to 300, in 1662 to 400, in 1694 to 700, in 1710 to 800, in 1771 to 1000, and in 1802 to 1100. In imitation of our Hackney Coaches, Nicholas Sauvage introduced the Fiacres at Paris, in the year 1650. The hammer-cloth is an ornamental covering of the coach-box. Mr. S. Pegge says, "The Coachman formerly used to carry a hammer, pincers, a few nails, &c. in a leathern pouch hanging to his box, and this cloth was devised for the hiding of them from public view." See Pegge's "Anonymiana," p. 181.

It is said that the sum of £1500, arising from the duty on Hackney Coaches, was applied in part of the expense in rebuilding Temple Bar.

JAILOR.

PLATE VII.

THOSE persons who remember old Newgate, the Gate House at Westminster, and other places of confinement, will recollect how small and inconvenient those buildings were, and must acknowledge the very great improvements as to the extensive accommodation of all our Prisons, not only in London, but in almost every county in England; and for these very great improvements no one could have stood more forward than the benevolent Howard. It is to him the public owe extensiveness of building, separations in the prisons for the various criminals, and most liberal supply of fresh water. Since his time there have been few jail distempers, as the prisoners have spacious yards to walk in, and by thus being exposed to fresh air are kept free from fevers and other disorders incidental to places of confinement. Let any one who recollects old Newgate survey the present structure, and he will be highly gratified with the respectable order kept up in that edifice. In some of the counties the jails may be looked upon as asylums, for neatness and good management, particularly that of Cambridge, where, instead of the whole of the prisoners for every sort of crime being huddled together in the tower of the Castle, they have now a building which affords separate apartments for men, women, and children, and this on the most elevated spot, commanding views of the adjacent country from every window. Whoever has visited Chelmsford Jail must have been delighted with its humane and sensible construction. Those who do not recollect the old prisons will, upon an inspection of Fox's Book of Martyrs, perceive in the Prisons of Lambeth Palace, the Bishop of London's House, Aldersgate Street, &c. how very small and confined those prisons were, having been not above eight feet square, with low ceilings and hardly an opening to let in the light. In addition to these miseries each room had its stocks, in which the prisoners were placed. The residences of our sovereigns in former days had likewise their prisons. Three of these were in the old palace of Westminster, viz. Heaven, Purgatory, and Hell. Heaven was a place where, if the prisoners could afford to pay, they had accommodations. Purgatory was a place with a ceiling so low that they could not walk without bending the head into the chest; and Hell was a dungeon with little or no light, where they had only bread and water. The pump lately standing in the street close by the Exchequer Coffee House, and now carried to the opposite side of the way, was the pump of this last prison, and to this day goes under the appellation of "Hell Pump."

To the credit of present manners, our modern jailors are in general men of feeling, and wherever it is discovered that they act with cruelty they are immediately dismissed from their office. This was not the case in former days, for they were in general the most hard-hearted of men, and callous even to the distresses of the aged, and crying infant at the breast.

The following Plate, pourtraying a Jailor of those times, will sufficiently convey an idea of the morose gluttony of such a character. It was copied from a rare tract, entitled, "Essayes and Characters of a Prison and Prisoners, by Geffray Mynshul, of Grayes Inne, Gent. with new additions, 1638." On the right side of the figure is written, "Those that keepe me, I keepe; if can, will still." On the left hand, "Hee's a true Jaylor strips the Divell in ill." The following extracts from this curious work will shew the estimation in which the author held a Jailor:

"As soone as thou commest before the gate of the prison, doe but think thou art entring into Hell, and it will extenuate somewhat of thy misery, for thou shalt be sure not only to find Hell, but fiends and ugly monsters, which with continuall torments will afflict thee; for at the gate there stands Cerberus, a man in shew, but a dogge in nature, who at thy entrance will fawne upon thee, bidding thee welcome, in respect of the golden croft which he must have cast him; then he opens the doore with all gentlenes, shewing thee the way to misery is very facile, and being once in, he shuts it with such fury, that it makes the foundation shake, and the doore and windows so barricadoed, that a man so loseth himself with admiration that he can hardly finde the way out and be a sound man.

"Now for the most part your porter is either some broken cittizen who hath plaid jack of all trades, some pander, broker, or hangman, that hath plaid the knave with all men; and for the more certainty his emblem is a red beard, to which sacke hath made his nose cousin-german.

"If marble-hearted Jaylors were so haplesse happy as to be mistaken, and be made Kings, they would, instead of iron to their grates, have barres made of men's ribs, Death should stand at doore for porter, and the Divell every night come gingling of keyes, and rapping at doores to lock men up.

"The broker useth to receive pawnes, but when he hath the feathers he lets the bird flye at liberty: but the Jaylor when he hath beene plum'd with the prisoner's pawnes, detaines him for his last morsell.

"He feedes very strangely, for some say he eates cloakes, hats, shirts, beds, and bedsteds, brasse, or pewter, or gold rings, plate, and the like; but I say he is in his dyet more greedy than Cannibals, for they eate but some parts of a man, but this devoures the whole body. The tenne-peny and nine-peny

26

ordinaries should never bee in the Fleet, Gatehouse, or the two infernal Compters, for Hunger would lay the cloth, and Famine would play the leane-fac'd serving-man to take away the trenchers."

A PRISON BASKET-MAN.

PLATE VIII.

THIS Plate exhibits one of those men who were sent out to beg broken meat for the poor prisoners. It was copied from one of the sets published by Overton in the reign of King Charles the Second. This custom, which perhaps was as ancient as our Religious Houses, has been long done away by an allowance of meat and bread having been made to those prisoners who are destitute of support.

It was the business of such men to claim the attention of the public by their cry of "Some broken breade and meate for ye poore prisonors! for the Lord's sake pitty the poore!" This mendicant for the prisoners is also noticed with the following London Cries, in a play entitled, "Tarquin and Lucrece," viz. "A Marking Stone." "Breade and Meate for the poor Prisoners." "Rock Samphire." "A Hassoc for your pew, or a Pesocke to thrust your feet in." In former days the passenger was solicited in the most melancholy and piteous manner by the poor prisoners. A tin box was lowered by a wire from the windows of their prisons into the street, so as to be even with the eye of the passenger. The confined persons, in hoarse, but sometimes solemn tones, solicited the public to "Remember the poor prisoners!" Not many persons can now recollect the tin boxes of this description, suspended from the Gatehouse at Westminster, and under the gloomy postern of old Newgate; but the custom was till lately continued at the Fleet Prison: where a box of the above description was put out from a grated window, even with the street, where one of the prisoners, who took it by turns, implored the public to "Remember the poor Insolvent Debtors;" but as the person was seen, and so near the street, the impression made on the passenger had not that gloomy and melancholy air of supplication as when uttered from a hollow voice at a distance, and in darkness; so that hundreds passed by without attending to the supplicant.

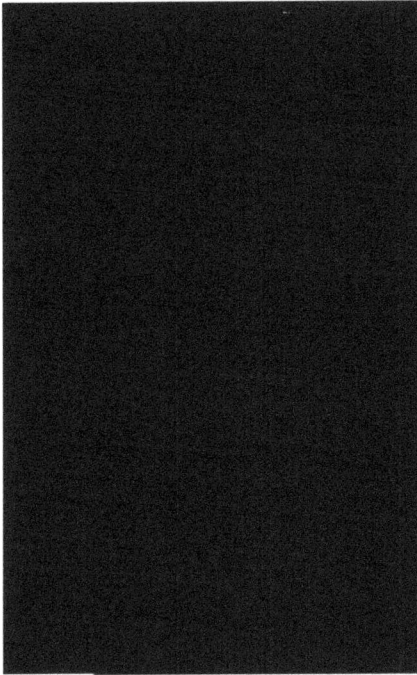

Few of those gentlemen who come into office of Sheriff with a dashing spirit quit their station without doing some, and, indeed, to do them justice, essential service to the community. Sir Richard Phillips, when sheriff, established the poor boxes put up on the outside of Newgate, with a restriction that they should be opened in the presence of the Sheriffs, and distributed by them to the poor prisoners, so that there could be no embezzlement, and the donations thus rendered certain of being equally and fairly divided among the proper objects, according to their distressing claims.

The following extract is from a work published by Mr. Murray in 1815, entitled, "Collections relative to Systematic Relief of the Poor," and which perhaps may be the earliest notice of mendicants by proxy. Plutarch notices a Rhodian custom, which is particularly mentioned by Phœnix of Colophon, a writer of Iambics, who describes certain men going about to collect donations for the crow, and singing or saying,

> "My good worthy masters, a pittance bestow,
> Some oatmeal, or barley, or wheat, for the crow;
> A loaf, or a penny, or e'en what you will,

As fortune your pockets may happen to fill.
From the poor man a grain of his salt may suffice,
For your crow swallows all and is not over nice.
And the man who can now give his grain and no more,
May another day give from a plentiful store.
Come, my lad, to the door, Plutus nods to our wish,
And our sweet little mistress comes out with a dish.
She gives us her figs, and she gives us a smile,
Heav'n bless her! and guard her from sorrow and guile,
And send her a husband of noble degree,
And a boy to be danced on his grand-daddy's knee;
And a girl like herself, all the joy of her mother,
Who may one day present her with just such another.
God bless your dear hearts all a thousand times o'er,
Thus we carry our crow-song to door after door;
Alternately chaunting we ramble along,
And we treat all who give, or give not, with a song."

And the song ever concludes:

"My good worthy masters, your pittance bestow,
Your bounty, my good worthy mistresses, throw.
Remember the crow! he is not over nice;
Do but give as you can, and the gift will suffice."

RAT-CATCHER.

PLATE IX.

THERE are two kinds of rats known in this country, the black, which was formerly very common, but is now rarely seen, being superseded by the large brown kind, commonly called the Norway rat. The depredations committed by this little animal, which is about nine inches long, can be well attested by the millers and feeders of poultry, as in addition to its mischief it frequently carries off large quantities to its hiding place.

In 1813 the following computation was made: "The annual value of the European Empire cannot be less than 25 millions sterling, and of this at least one fiftieth part, upon the lowest calculation, is eaten and destroyed by rats and mice; the public loss therefore is at least 500,000*l. per annum*, exclusive of the damage done in ships, in store houses, and buildings of every kind."

The bite of the rat is keen, and the wound it inflicts painful and difficult to heal, owing to the form of its teeth, which are long, sharp, and irregular. It produces from twelve to eighteen at a litter, and were it not that these animals destroy each other, the country would soon be overrun with them.

Mr. Bewick observes, "It is a singular fact in the history of these animals, that the skins of such of them as have been devoured in their holes, have frequently been found curiously turned inside out, every part being completely inverted, even to the ends of the toes."

In addition to this remark of Mr. Bewick, it may be mentioned, that though the destruction of rats is so great among themselves, yet they are in some degree attached to each other, and have even their sports and pastimes. It is well known that a herd of rats will be defenders of their own holes, and that when a strange brood trespass upon their premises, they are sure to be set upon and devoured. They are active as the squirrel, and will, like that animal, sit up and eat their food. They play at hide and seek with each other, and have been known to hide themselves in the folds of linen, where they have remained quite still until their playmates have discovered them, in the same manner as kittens. Most readers will recollect the fable where a young mouse suggests that the cat should have a bell fastened to his neck, so that his companions might be aware of his approach. This idea was scouted by one of their wiseheads, who asked who was to tye the bell round the cat's neck? This experiment has actually been tried upon a rat. A bell was fastened round his neck, and he was replaced in his hole, with full expectation of his frightening the rest away, but it turned out that instead of their continuing to be alarmed at his approach, he was heard for the space of a year to frolick and scamper with them. In China the Jugglers cause their rats and mice to dance together to music, and oblige them to take leaps as we teach our cats. The following is a copy of a handbill distributed in Cornhill a few years ago:

"A most wonderful Rat, the greatest natural curiosity ever seen in London.

"A gigantic Female Rat, taken near Somerset House: it is truly worthy the inspection of the curious, its length being three feet three inches, and its weight ten pounds three quarters; and twenty-four inches in circumference. Any lady or gentleman purchasing goods to the amount of one shilling or upwards, will have an opportunity of seeing it gratis, at No. 5, Sweeting's Alley, Cornhill."

Rats were made use of as a plague, see 1st Book of Kings, chap. v. Nich. Poussin painted this subject, which has been engraved by Stephen Picart of Rome, 1677.

In a curious tract, entitled "Green's Ghost," published in 1626, Watermen are nicknamed water-rats; an appellation also bestowed on pirates by the immortal bard of Avon.

The down of the musk-rat of Canada is used in the manufacture of hats. From the tail of the Muscovy musk-rat is extracted a kind of musk, very much resembling the genuine sort, and their skins are frequently laid among clothes to preserve them from moths.

"The musk-rat is of all the small species larger and whiter than the common. He exhales, as he moves, a very strong smell of musk, which penetrates even the best inclosures. If, for example, one of the animals pass over a row of bottles, the liquor they contain will be so strongly scented with musk that it cannot be drunk. The writer has known tons of wine touched by them so strongly infected, that it was with the greatest difficulty, and by a variety of process, that they could be purged of this smell. These rats are a great plague to all the country, and, if they once get into a cellar or magazine, are very hard to destroy. Cats will not venture to attack them, for fear probably of being suffocated by the smell; nor will the European terrier hurt them." See Les Hindous, par E. Baltazard Solvyns, tom. 4. Paris, 1812, folio.

The Norwegians of late years have the following effectual mode of getting rid of their rats:

They singe the hair of one of them over a fire, and then let it loose; the stench is so offensive to his comrades that they all immediately quit the house, and are eventually destroyed by combating with other broods. This expedient has become so general, that Norway is relieved of one of its greatest pests. The above method was communicated to the writer by a native, who wondered that our farmers had not adopted it.

It appears in that very masterly set of etchings by Simon Guillain, or Guilini, from drawings made by Annibal Caracci, of the Cries of Bologna, published in 1646, that the Rat-catcher had representations of rats and mice painted upon a square cloth fastened to a pole like a flag, which he carried across his shoulder.

The Chinese Rat and Mouse-killer carries a cat in a bag. In Ben Jonson's time, the King's most excellent Mole-catcher lived in Tothill Street.

MARKING STONES.

PLATE X.

THE rare wood-cut, from which the present etching was made, is one of the curious set of twelve figures engraved in wood of the time of James the First. Under the figure are the following lines:

> "Buy Marking Stones, Marking Stones buy,
> Much profit in their use doth lie:
> I've marking stones of colour red,
> Passing good,—or else black lead."

The cry of Marking Stones is also noticed in the play of "Tarquin and Lucrece." These Marking Stones, as the verses above state, are either of a red colour, or composed of black lead. They were used in marking of linen, so that washing could not take the mark out. Every one knows that water will not take effect upon black lead, particularly if the stick of that material, which is denominated "a Marking Stone," be heated before it be stamped. The stone, of a red colour, was probably of a material impregnated with the red called "ruddle," a colour never to be washed out. It is used by the graziers for the marking of their sheep, is of an oily nature, and made in immense quantities, for the use of graziers, at the Ruddle Manufactory, near the Nine Elms, on the Battersea Road. It was a red known in the reign of Edward the Third, and much used by the painters employed in the decorations of St. Stephen's Chapel, Westminster.

About fifty years ago it was the custom of those persons who let lodgings in St. Giles's, above the Two-penny admission, where sheets were afforded at sixpence the night, to stamp their linen with sticks of marking stones of ruddle, with the words "Stop Thief," so that, if stolen, the thief should at once be detected and detained. For this, and many other curious particulars respecting the lowest classes of the inhabitants of St. Giles in the Fields, the writer is much indebted to his truly respectable friend, the late William Packer, Esq. of Charlotte Street, Bloomsbury, and afterwards of Great Baddow, in Essex, who was born, and resided for the great part of his life, upon the spot. For the honour of this gentleman's family, it may be here acknowledged that his father, who was also a truly respectable man, was one of the promoters of the building of Middlesex Hospital, which, before the erection of the present building, was an establishment held in Windmill Street, leading from Tottenham Court Road to Percy Chapel, in Charlotte

Street, Rathbone Place. The house which the Hospital occupied, standing on the South side of the street, has since been made use of as a French charity school.

BUY A BRUSH, OR A TABLE BOOK.

PLATE XI.

THE Engraving from which the accompanying Plate was copied was one of a set published by Overton, but without date. Judging from the dress, it must have been made either in the reign of King James the First or in that of the succeeding monarch. The inscription over the figure is, "Buy a Brush or a Table Book." The floors were not wetted, but rubbed dry, even until they bore a very high polish, particularly when it was the fashion to inlay staircases and floors of rooms with yellow, black, and brown woods. On the landing places of the great staircase in the house built by Lord Orford, now the Grand Hotel, at the end of King Street in Covent Garden, such inlaid specimens are still remaining, in a beautiful state of preservation. There are many houses of the nobility where the floors consist of small pieces of oak arranged in tessellated forms. The room now occupied by the servants in waiting, and that part of the house formerly a portion of the old gallery, at Cleveland House, St. James's; the floors of the state rooms of Montagu House, now the British Museum; and the floor of the Library in St. Paul's Cathedral, all retain their tessellated forms. These floors were rubbed by the servants, who wore brushes on their feet, and they were, and indeed are, so highly polished, in some of the country mansions, that in some instances they are dangerous to walk upon. This mode of dry-rubbing rooms by affixing the brush to the feet, is still practised in France, chiefly by men-servants.

The Table Book is of very ancient use. Shakspeare thus notices it in his play of Hamlet:

> *Ham.* My tables: meet it is
> I set it down.

It was a book consisting of several small pieces of slate set in frames of wood, fastened together with hinges, and closed, as a book for the pocket: for a representation of one, with a pencil attached to a string, as used in 1565, see Douce's "Illustrations of Shakspeare and of Ancient Manners," vol. II. p. 227. It was taken, says that writer, from Gesner's Treatise De rerum fossilium figuris, &c. Tigur. 1565. The Almanacs of that time likewise contained tables of a composition like asses skin. One of these was in the possession of Mr. Douce.

It is a very curious fact that the farmers, graziers, and horse dealers, use at this day a Table Book consisting of slates bound in wood, with a pencil attached to it, exactly of the same make as that referred to as used in 1565, and such are now regularly sold at the toy shops. We may conclude that persons in the higher ranks of life used sheets of ivory put together as a book, for we frequently meet with such, elegantly adorned with clasps, of very old workmanship.

Howell, in his "Familiar Letters," 4to. p. 7, published 1645, says, "This return of Sir Walter Raleigh from Guiana puts me in minde of a facetious tale I read lately in Italian, (for I have a little of that language already,) how Alphonso King of Naples sent a Moor, who had been his captive a long time, to Barbary, to buy horses, and to return by such a time. Now there was about the King a kinde of buffon or jester who had a Table Book, wherein he was used to register any absurdity, or impertinence, or merry passage, that happened about the Court. That day the Moor was dispatched for Barbary, the said jester waiting upon the King at supper, the King called for his journall, and askt what he had observed that day; thereupon he produced his Table Book, and amongst other things he read how Alphonso King of Naples had sent Beltran the Moor, who had been a long time his prisoner, to Morocco, his own country, with so many thousand crowns to buy horses. The King asked him 'why he inserted that?' 'Because,' said he, 'I think he will never come back to be a prisoner again, and so you have lost both man and money.' 'But, if he do come, then your jest is marr'd,' quoth the King. 'No, sir; for if he return, I will blot out your name, and put him in for a fool.'"

FIRE-SCREENS.

PLATE XII.

THE next plate is a copy from the same set of prints from which the preceding one was taken, and has the following inscription engraved above it:

"I have screenes if you desier,
To keepe y^r butey from ye fire."

It appears from the extreme neatness of this man, and the goods which he exhibits for sale, that they were of a very superior quality, probably of foreign manufacture, and possibly from Leghorn, from whence hats similar to those on his head were first brought into England. These Leghorn hats were originally imported and sold by our Turners, who generally had the Leghorn hat for their sign. England certainly can boast of superiority in almost every description of manufacture, over those of most parts of the world; but it never successfully rivalled the Basket-makers and Willow-workers of France and Holland, either for bleaching or weaving; nor perhaps is it possible for any skill to exceed that of the French in their present mode of making baskets and other such ware. Even the children's rattles of the Dutch and French, surpass anything of the kind made in this country. The willow is common in most parts of Holland, so that they have a great choice of a selection of wood, and the females are taught the art of twisting it at a very early age. It must be acknowledged, that the natives of Hudson's Bay are very curious workers of baskets and other useful articles made of the barks of trees, and even the most uncultivated nations often display exquisite neatness in their modes of making them. The French carry their basket ware either in small barrows or in little carts, and sell them at so cheap a rate, by reason of the few duties they have to pay to Government, that it would be impossible for an Englishman, were he master of the art of producing them, to sell them for less than ten times the sum.

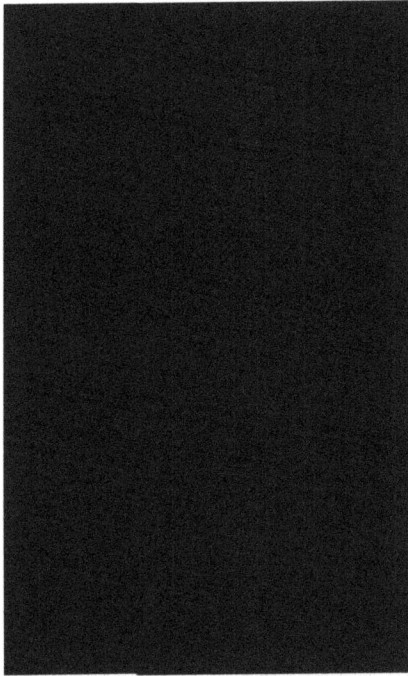

That very wonderful people the Chinese probably were the first who thought of hand-screens to protect the face from the sun. We find them introduced in their earliest delineations of costume. The feathered fans of our Elizabeth might occasionally have been used as fire screens, in like manner as those now imported from the East Indies, also composed of feathers, and which frequently adorn our chimney pieces. It is possible, however, that as our vendor of Fire-screens has particularly acquainted us with the use of his screens, they might have been the first that were introduced decidedly for that purpose.

SAUSAGES.

PLATE XIII.

THE female vendor of Sausages exhibited in the following Plate, is of the time of Charles II. and has here been preferred to a similar character belonging to the preceding reign, her dress and general appearance being far more picturesque. Under the original print are the following lines:

> "Who buys my Sausages! Sausages fine!
> I ha' fine Sausages of the best,
> As good they are as e'er was eat,
> If they be finely drest.
> Come, Mistris, buy this daintie pound,
> About a Capon rost them round."

Almost every county has some peculiar mode of making sausages, but as to their general appearance they are tied up in links. There are several sorts which have for many years upheld their reputation, such as those made at Bewdley in Oxfordshire, at Epping, and at Cambridge, places particularly famous for them. The sausages from Bewdley, Epping, and Cambridge, are mostly sold by the poulterers, who are in general very attentive in having them genuine. They are brought to Leadenhall, Newgate, and other markets, neatly put up in large flat baskets, similar to those in which fresh butter is sent to town. The Oxford gentlemen frequently present their London friends with some of the sausage meat put up in neat brown pans; this is fried in cakes, and is remarkably good.

The pork-shops of Fetter Lane have been for upwards of 150 years famous for their sausages; indeed the pork-shops throughout London are principally supported by a most extensive sale of sausages.

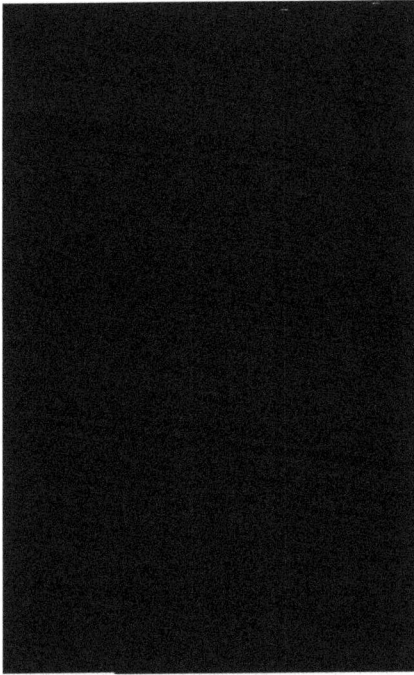

Ben Jonson, in his play of Bartholomew Fair, exhibits sausage stalls, their contents being prime articles of refreshment at that very ancient festival. In a very curious tract, entitled, "A Narrative of the Life of Mrs. Charlotte Charke, (*youngest daughter* of Colley Cibber, Esq.) written by herself, the second edition, printed for W. Reeve, in Fleet Street, 1759," the authoress, after experiencing some of the most curious vicissitudes, in the midst of her greatest distress, says, "I took a neat lodging in a street facing *Red Lyon Square*, and wrote a letter to Mr. *Beard*, intimating to him the sorrowful plight I was in; and, in a quarter of an hour after, my request was obligingly complied with by that worthy gentleman, whose bounty enabled me to set forward to *NewgateMarket*, and bought a considerable quantity of pork at the best hand, which I converted into sausages, and with my daughter set out laden with each a burden as weighty as we could well bear; which, not having been used to luggages of that nature, we found extremely troublesome. But *Necessitas non habeat legem*, we were bound to that or starve.

"Thank heaven, our loads were like Æsop's, when he chose to carry the bread, which was the weightiest burden, to the astonishment of his fellow-travellers; not considering that his wisdom preferred it, because he was sure it would lighten as it went: so did ours, for as I went only where I was known, I soon disposed, among my friends, of my whole cargo; and was happy in the thought, that the utmost excesses of my misfortunes had no worse effect on me, than an industrious inclination to get a small livelihood, without shame or reproach; though the Arch-Dutchess of our family, who would not have relieved me with a halfpenny roll or a draught of small-beer, imputed this to me as a crime; I suppose she was possessed with the same dignified sentiments Mrs. Peachum is endowed with, and THOUGHT THE HONOUR OF THEIR FAMILY WAS CONCERNED; if so, she knew the way to have prevented the disgrace, and in a humane, justifiable manner, have preserved her own from that taint of cruelty I doubt she will never overcome."

The wretched vendors of sausages, who cared not what they made them of, such as those about forty years back who fried them in cellars in St. Giles's, and under gateways in Drury Lane, Field Lane, commonly called "Food and Raiment Alley, or Thieving Lane, alias Sheep's Head Alley," with all its courts and ramifications of Black Boy Alley, Saffron Hill, Bleeding Heart Yard, and Cow Cross, were continually persecuting their unfortunate neighbours, to whom they were as offensive as the melters of tallow, bone burners, soap boilers, or cat-gut cleaners. This "Food and Raiment Alley," so named from the cook and old clothes shops, was in former days so dangerous to go through, that it was scarcely possible for a person to possess his watch or his handkerchief by the time he had passed this ordeal of infamy; and it is a fact, that a man after losing his pocket-handkerchief, might, on his immediate return through the Lane, see it exposed for sale, and purchase it at half the price it originally cost him, of the mother of the young gentleman who had so dextrously deprived him of it. Watches were, as they are now in many places in London, immediately put into the crucible to evade detection.

NEW ELEGY.

PLATE XIV.

T HIS figure was drawn and etched by the writer from an itinerant vendor of Elegies, Christmas Carols, and Love Songs. His father and grandfather had followed the same calling.

When this man was asked what particular event he recollected, his information was principally confined to the Elegies he had sold. He seemed anxious, however, to inform the public that in the year 1753 the quartern loaf was sold at fourpence halfpenny, mutton was two-pence halfpenny a pound, that porter was then three-pence a pot, and that the National Debt was twenty-four millions. Notwithstanding this man's memory served him in the above particulars, which perhaps he had repeated so often that he could not forget them, yet he positively did not know his age; he said he never troubled his head with that, for that his father told him if he only mentioned the year of his birth any scholar could tell it. His father, he observed, cried the Elegy of that notorious magistrate Sir Thomas de Veil,[13] which went through nine editions, as there was hardly a thief or strumpet that did not purchase one.

Hogarth is supposed to have introduced this magistrate in his "Woman swearing a Child to a grave Citizen." In his Plate of "Night," the drunken Freemason has also been supposed to be Sir Thomas de Veil. This man had rendered himself so obnoxious by his intrigues with women, and his bare-faced partialities in screening the opulent, that the executors, who were afraid of the coffin being torn to pieces by the mob, privately conveyed it to a considerable distance from Bow Street by three o'clock in the morning.

It was formerly not only the custom to print Elegies on the great people, but on all those in the lowest class of life who had rendered themselves conspicuous as public characters. Indeed we may recollect the Elegies to the memory of Sam House, the political tool of Mr. Fox among the vulgar part of his voters, and also that to the memory of Henry Dimsdale, the muffin man, nicknamed Sir Harry Dimsdale, the Mayor of Garratt, who succeeded the renowned Sir Jeffrey Dunstan, commonly called Old Wigs, from his being a purchaser of those articles. The last Elegy was to the memory of the lamented Princess Charlotte, and it was then that the portrait of the above-mentioned Elegy-vender was taken.

With respect to his Christmas Carols, he said they had varied almost every year in their bordered ornaments; and the writer regrets the loss of a collection of Christmas Carols from the time of this man's grandfather, which, had he been fortunate enough to have made his drawing of the above vendor only three days before, he could have purchased for five shillings. The collectors in general of early English woodcuts may not be aware that there were printed Christmas Carols so early as Queen Mary the First. The writer, when a boy, detected several patches of one that had been fastened against the wall of the Chapel of St. Edmond in Westminster Abbey. It had marginal woodcut illustrations, which reminded him of those very interesting blocks engraved for "Hollinshed's Chronicle." It appears that some part of this curious Carol was remaining when Mr. Malcolm wrote his description of the above Chapel for his Work on London. (Vol. I. p. 144.)

Love Songs, however old they might be, were pronounced by our Elegy-vender to be always saleable among the country people. Robert Burton, in his "Anatomy of Melancholy," part 3, sect. 2, speaking of love songs, says, "As Carmen, Boyes, and Prentises, when a new song is published with us, go singing that new tune still in the streets, they continually acted that tragical part of *Perseus*, and in every man's mouth was *O, Cupid! Prince of Gods and Men!* pronouncing still like stage-players, *O, Cupid!* they were so possessed all with that rapture, and thought of that pathetical love speech, they could not a long time after forget, or drive it out of their minds, but, *O, Cupid! Prince of Gods and Men!* was ever in their mouths."

In the second volume, page 141, of Shenstone's Works, the author says, "The ways of ballad singers, and the cries of halfpenny pamphlets, appeared so extremely humourous, from my lodgings in Fleet Street, that it gave me pain to observe them without a companion to partake. For, alas! laughter is by no means a solitary entertainment."

ALL IN FULL BLOOM.

PLATE XV.

THE repeated victories gained by England over her enemies, and her unbounded liberality to them when in distress, not only by her pecuniary contributions, but by allowing this country to be their general seat of refuge during their own commotions, encouraged the ignorant among them still to continue in their belief that the streets of our great city were paved with gold. The consequence has been, that the number of idle foreigners who have been tempted to quit their homes have increased the vagrants who now infest our streets with their learned mice and chattering monkies, to the great annoyance of those passengers who do not contribute to their exhibitions; for it is their practice not only to let the animals loose to the extent of a long string, but to encourage them to run up to the balconies, oftentimes to the great terror of the families who have disregarded their impertinent importunities.

The writer of this work once reprimanded a French organist for throwing his dancing mice upon a nursery maid, because she did not contribute to reward him for the amusement they afforded her young master.

Among the various foreigners thus visiting us to make their fortunes is Anatony Antonini, a native of Lucca in Tuscany, from which place come most of those fellows who carry images and play the organ about our streets. He is exhibited in the annexed etching, with his show board of artificial flowers, "All in full bloom!" constructed of silk and paper, with wires for their stalks. The birds perched on their branches are made of wax, cast from plaster of Paris moulds. They are gaily painted and varnished, and in some instances so thin that their bodies are quite transparent.

The custom of casting figures in wax is very ancient, especially in Roman Catholic countries, where they represent the Virgin and Child and other sacred subjects as articles of devotion for the poorer sort of people who cannot afford to purchase those carved in ivory. It is said that Mrs. Salmon's exhibition of wax-work in Fleet Street, whose sign of a Salmon was noticed by Addison in the Spectator, owes its origin to a schoolmistress, the wife of one of Henry the Seventh's body guards. This woman distributed little wax dolls as rewards to the most deserving of her scholars, and, it is reported, brought the art from Holland.

Some few years ago a very interesting exhibition of artificial flowers was made in Suffolk Street, Charing Cross, by a female of the name of Dards, who had most ingeniously produced many hundreds of the most beautiful flowers from fishes' bones, which, when warm, she twisted into shapes. The leaves were made from the skins of soles, eels, &c. which were stained with proper colours. The flowers of the lily of the valley were represented by the bones of the turbot which contain the brain, and were so complete a deception that they were often mistaken for a bunch of the real flowers. This exhibition did not answer the expectation of Mrs. Dards, as few persons could believe it possible that fishes' bones were capable of being converted into articles of such elegance.

The ribs of the whale were frequently erected at the entrances of our tea gardens, and many remained within memory at the Spring Gardens, Chelsea; Cromwell's Gardens, Brompton; Copenhagen House, &c. The inhabitants of the coast of Mechran, who live mostly upon fish, build their houses of the rudest materials, frequently of the large fish that are thrown on the shore.

About thirty-five years ago, there was another very singular "All blooming" man, a black with wooden legs, who carried natural flowers about the streets. His trick to claim attention was remarkable, as he generally contrived to startle passengers with his last vociferation. His cry was, "All blooming! blooming! blooming!!! all alive! alive!! alive!!!"

It is notable fact that blacks, when they become public characters in our streets, as they are more or less masters of humour, display their wit to the amusement of the throng, and thereby make a great deal of money. They always invent some novelty to gain the attention of the crowd. One of these fellows, under the name of Peter, held a dialogue between himself and his master, nearly to the following effect:

Master. "Oh, Peter, you very bad boy; you no work; you lazy dog."—*Peter.* "Oh massa, 'give me this time, Peter Peter do so no more; Peter Peter no more run away."—This duet he accompanied with a guitar, in so humourous a style, that he was always sure to please his audience. He would, at the completion of his song, pass himself through a hoop, and, while holding a stick, twist his arms round his body in a most extraordinary manner. His last performance was that of placing his head backwards between his legs and picking up a pin with his mouth from the ground, without any assistance from hands, his arms being folded round his body before he commenced his exhibition.

The Chinese florist carries his flowers in two flat baskets suspended from a pole placed across his shoulders, the whole being similar to our scales with their beam.

OLD CHAIRS TO MEND.

PLATE XVI.

THE Plate exhibits the figure of Israel Potter, one of the oldest menders of chairs now living, who resides in Compton's Buildings, Burton Crescent, and sallies forth by eight o'clock in the morning, not with a view of getting chairs to mend; for, from the matted mass of dirty rushes which have sometimes been thrown across his shoulders for months together, without ever being once opened, it must be concluded that his cry of "Old chairs to mend" avails him but little; the fact is, that like many other itinerants, he goes his rounds and procures broken meat and subsistence thus early in the morning for his daily wants.

The seating of chairs with rushes cannot be traced further back than a century, as the chairs in common as well as public use in the reign of Queen Anne had cane seats and backs. Previously to that time, and even in the days of Elizabeth, cushion seats and stuffed backs were made use of.

In the reign of Henry the Eighth, and in remoter times, the chairs were made entirely of wood, and in many instances the backs were curiously carved, either with figures, grotesque heads, or foliage. Most of the early chairs had arms for supporting elbows, and which were also carved. In the Archæologia, published by the Society of Antiquaries, several representations of ancient chairs are given.[14] Of the Royal thrones, the reader will find a curious succession, from the time of Edward the Confessor to that of James the First, exhibited in the great seals of England, representations of most of which have been published by Speed in his History of Great Britain, and in Sandford's Genealogical History of England.

The cry of "Old Chairs to mend!" is frequently uttered with great clearness, and occasionally with some degree of melody. Suett, the late facetious Comedian, took the cry of "Old Chairs to mend," in an interlude, entitled, the "Cries of London," performed some years since in the Little Theatre in the Haymarket, and repeated the old lines of

> "Old Chairs to mend! Old Chairs to mend!
> If I had the money that I could spend,
> I never would cry Old Chairs to mend."[15]

The late John Bannister, who performed in the same piece, took the cry of "Come here's your scarlet ware, long and strong scarlet garters, twopence a pair, twopence a pair, twopence a pair!" which was a close imitation of a little fellow who made a picturesque appearance about the streets with his long scarlet garters streaming from the end of a pole.

The late eccentric actor Baddeley, who left a sum of money to purchase a cake to be eaten by his successors every Twelfth Night, in the Green-room of Drury Lane Theatre, took the cry of "Come buy my shrimps, come buy my shrimps, prawns, very large prawns, a wine-quart a penny periwinkles."

The late Dr. Owen informed the present writer that he had heard that the author of "God save the King" caught the tones either from a man who cried "Old Chairs to mend," or from another who cried "Come buy my door-mats;" and it is well known that one of Storace's most favourite airs in "No Song no Supper," was almost wholly constructed from a common beggar's chaunt.

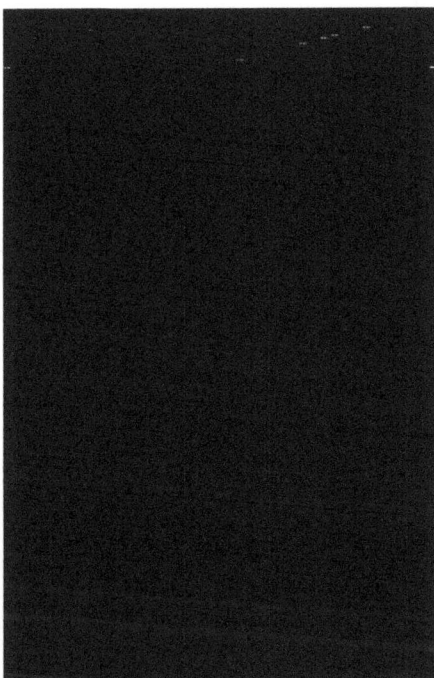

THE BASKET-MAKER.

PLATE XVII.

THE man whose figure affords the subject of the next Plate is a journeyman Prickle-maker, and works in a cellar on the western side of the Haymarket. A prickle is a basket used by the wine-merchants for their empty bottles; it is made of osiers unpeeled and in their natural state, and the basket is made loose with open work, so that when it is filled with bottles it may ride easy in the wine-merchant's caravan, and without the least risk of breaking them. The maker of prickles begins the formation of the bottom of the basket by placing the osier twigs in the form of a star flat upon the ground; he then with another twig commences his weaving by twisting it under and over the ends of the twigs which meet in the centre of the star, and so he goes on to the extent of the circumference of the intended prickle; he then bends up the surrounding twigs, which are in a moist state, and binds them in the middle and the top, and thus the prickle is finished. The formation of hampers for wine-merchants' sieves, and baskets for the gardeners and fishmongers, and indeed that of all other basket work, is begun in the same way as the prickle. The basket-maker is seated upon a broad flat stage consisting of at least four boards clamped together, touching the ground at one end, on which his feet are placed, but elevated about six feet. Upon the end where he is seated free air passes under him, and thus he takes less cold from the ground of the cellar.

In Lapland large baskets are made by two persons, a man and a woman. Their mode of forming their baskets in every particular is similar to that of the English. On the banks of the Thames, from Fulham to Staines, there were formerly numerous basket-makers' huts, but opulent persons, anxious to have houses on those delightful spots, purchased the ground on the expiration of the leases, and erected fashionable villas on their site. The inducement for the basket-makers occupying the sides of the Thames, was the great supply of osiers or young willows which grow on the aits, particularly at Twickenham and Staines.

The usual price of each prickle is two shillings and three pence. Notwithstanding the numbers of osiers grown in this country, the produce is not sufficient, as an extensive importation of twigs is annually made from Holland, where immense quantities of baskets of every description are made. The Dutch are particularly neat and famous for their willow sieves, which find a ready market in every country.

The reader may probably be amused with a list of those trades exercised in Holland, which in their pronunciation and meaning resemble the same in this country, beginning with the

Sieve Maker,	which in Dutch is	Zeevmaker.
Baker		Bakker.
Scale Maker		Balansmaker.
Book Binder		Boekbinder.
Brewer		Broonwer.
Glass-blower		Glasblazer.
Glazier		Glazemaker.
Goldsmith		Goudsmit.
Musical Instrument Maker		Instrumentmaker.
Lanthorn Maker		Lantaarnmaker.
Paper Maker		Papiermaker.
Perriwig Maker		Paruikmaker.
Pump Maker		Pompemaker.
Potter,		Pottebaker.
Shoemaker		Schoenmaker.
Smith		Smit.
Schoolmaster		Schoolmeester.
Waggon Maker		Wagenmaker.
Weaver		Weever.
Sail Maker		Zailmaker.

THE POTTER.

PLATE XVIII.

AT about a mile from the back of Jack Straw's Castle, Hampstead Heath, through one of the prettiest lanes near London, the traveller will find that beautifully rural spot called "Child's Hill." This was the favourite walk of Gainsborough and Loutherburgh, both of whom occasionally had lodgings near the Heath for the purpose of study; and perhaps no place within one hundred miles of London affords better materials for the landscape painter's purpose than Hampstead Heath and its vicinity, particularly that most delightful spot above described, where the Pottery stands, which afforded the subject of the ensuing Plate.

At this Pottery, which is placed in a sequestered dell, the moulds used by the sugar bakers for casting their loaves of sugar in, are made. They are of different sizes, turned by the moulder, with the assistance of a boy, who is employed in keeping the lathe in motion. The clay is remarkably good, and burns to a rich red colour.

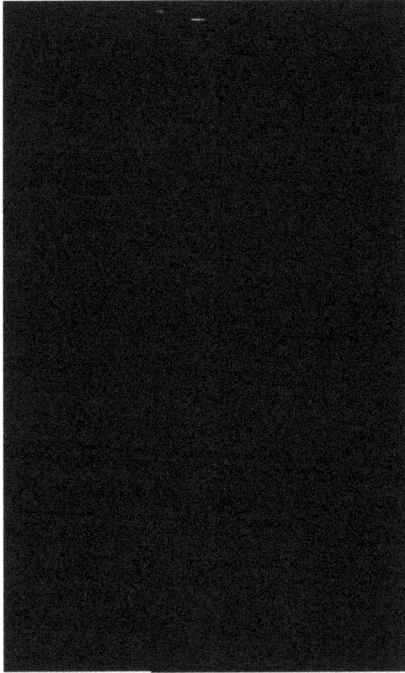

The following is a list of the places where sugar bakers' moulds are made, for they are not to be had at the Potteries in general; viz. that above-mentioned, at Child's Hill, near Hampstead Heath, in the parish of Hendon; one at Brentford; one at Clapham; one at Greenwich; three at Deptford; and two at Plumsted. Though the clay varies in texture, and likewise in colour in some slight degree, when baked, on almost every spot where a Pottery is erected, yet in no instance does it so peculiarly differ as at the Pottery in High Street, Lambeth, leading to Vauxhall. The clay principally used at that place is preferred by the sculptors for their models of busts, figures, and monuments. It never stains the fingers, and is of so beautiful a texture that all parts of the model may be executed with it, in the most minute degree of sharpness and spirit; and, when baked, it is not of that fiery red colour, like a tile, but approaches nearer to the tone of flesh, has a beautiful bloom with it, and is very similar, though not quite so dark, as those fine specimens of Terracottas in the Towneley Gallery, in the British Museum. The great sculptors Roubiliac and Rysbrach not only constantly preferred it, but brought it into general use among the artists.

At the Lambeth Pottery, the first imitations of the Dutch square white glazed tiles, decorated with figures of animals and other ornaments, painted in blue, and sometimes purple, were made in England. The fashion of thus decorating the backs of chimnies was introduced into this country soon after the arrival of William the Third, and continued till about fifty years ago. Chimnies thus ornamented are frequently to be met with in country houses, particularly in bed-rooms; but in London, where almost every body enters on a new fashion as soon as it appears, there are fewer specimens left. The chimney of the room in Bolt Court, in which Dr. Johnson died, was decorated with these tiles, most of the subjects of which were taken from Barlow's etchings of Æsop's Fables. Dinner services were produced of the same material, and painted blue or purple, like the above tiles. Sir James Thornhill, the painter of the pictures which adorn the dome of St. Paul's, and Paul Ferg, when young men, were employed at the Chelsea China manufactory, and there are specimens of plates and dishes painted by them now and then to be met with in the cabinets of the curious. At Mrs. Hogarth's sale (Sir James Thornhill's daughter), Lord Orford purchased twelve dinner plates painted by her father; the subjects were the Signs of the Zodiac, and they are preserved at Strawberry Hill.

In common ware, jugs, handbasins, dinner services, &c. are not painted, but printed, the mode of executing which is rather curious. Trees, hay-makers, cows, farm-houses, windmills, &c. are engraved on copper-plates, which are filled with blue colour (smalt). Impressions from them are taken on common blotting paper, through the rolling press. These impressions are immediately put on the earthen ware, and when the blotting-paper is dry, it is washed off, and the blue colour remains upon the dish, &c.

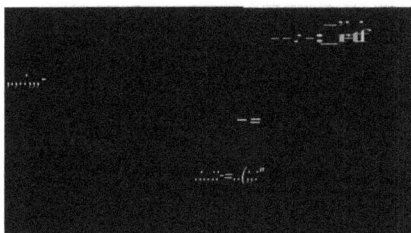

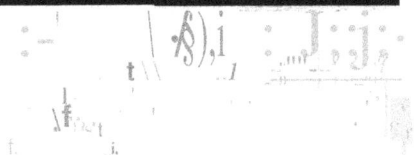

STAFFORDSHIRE WARE.

PLATE XIX.

OF all the tradesmen who supply the domestic table, there are none more frequently called upon than the earthen-ware man. In great families, where constant cooking is going on, the dust-bin seldom passes a day without receiving the accidents to which a scullery is liable, nor is there, upon an average, a private family in England that passes a week without some misfortune to their crockery. Many householders set down at least ten pounds a year for culinary restorations; so that the itinerant Staffordshire Ware vendor, exhibited in the following plate, is sure to sell something in every street he enters, particularly since that ware has been brought by water to Paddington, whence he and many others, who go all over the town to dispose of their stock in baskets, are regularly supplied; and in consequence of the safety and cheapness of the passage, they are enabled to dispose of their goods at so moderate a rate that they can undersell the regular shopkeeper.

Staffordshire is the principal place in England for the produce of earthen ware; the manufactories cover miles of land, and the minds of the people appear to be solely absorbed in their business. Coals cost them little but the labour of fetching; they work from twelve to fourteen hours a day, and those who choose to perform what they call over-time, are employed sixteen hours in each day. The men have for twelve hours in each day, being common time, seven shillings per week; the women four shillings, and the children, who turn the lathes, two shillings and sixpence. These people are so constantly at work and perpetually calling out "turn," when they wish it to go faster, to the boy who gives motion to the lathe, that it is said that those who fall into intoxication are sure, however drunk they may be, to call to the boy to turn, whether at work or not. There are men who make plates, others who make basins, &c.; and those who make jugs, tea and milkpots, have what they call handle-men, persons whose sole business it is to prepare the handles and stick them on. Their divisions of land, similar to banks or hedges, as well as their roads, for miles, are wholly constructed of their broken earthen-ware.

They have their regular packers, who pique themselves on getting in a dozen of plates more than usual in an immense basket.

When they meet with a clay that differs in colour from that they have been using, they will apply themselves most readily to make up a batch of plates, basins, or tea-cups, well knowing the public are pleased with a new colour;

and it is a curious fact that there are hundreds of varieties of tints produced from the different pits used by these Staffordshire manufactories. There are men whose business it is to glaze the articles, and others who pencil and put on the brown or white enamel with which the common yellow jug is streaked or ornamented. In the brown or yellow baking dishes used by the common people, the dabs of colour of brown and yellow are laid on by children, with sticks, in the quickest way imaginable. The profits of earthen-ware in general are very great, as indeed they ought to be, considering the brittleness of the article, and the number of accidents they are continually meeting with, as is demonstrated by their hedge-rows and roads.

An article that is sold for fourpence in London, costs but one penny at the manufactory.

-1:t:.:r

:./>

HARD METAL SPOONS TO SELL OR CHANGE.

PLATE XX.

W ILLIAM Conway, of Crab Tree Row, Bethnall Green, is the person from whom the following etching was made. He was born in 1752, in Worship Street, which spot was called Windmill Hill, and first started with or rather followed his father as an itinerant trader, forty-seven years ago. This man has walked on an average twenty-five miles a day six days in the week, never knew a day's illness, nor has he once slept out of his own bed. His shoes are made from the upper leather of old boots, and a pair will last him six weeks. He has eleven walks, which he takes in turn, and these are all confined to the environs of London; no weather keeps him within, and he has been wet and dry three times in a day without taking the least cold.

His spoons are made of hard metal, which he sells, or exchanges for the old ones he had already sold; the bag in which he carries them is of the thickest leather, and he has never passed a day without taking some money. His eyes are generally directed to the ground, and the greatest treasure he ever found was a one pound note; when quarters of guineas were in currency, he once had the good fortune to pick up one of them.

He never holds conversation with any other itinerant, nor does he drink but at his dinner; and it is pleasant to record, that Conway in his walks, by his great regularity, has acquired friends, several of whom employ him in small commissions.

His memory is good, and among other things he recollects Old Vinegar, a surly fellow so called from his brutal habits. This man provided sticks for the cudgel players, whose sports commenced on Easter Monday, and were much frequented by the Bridewell-boys. He was the maker of the rings for the boxers in Moorfields, and would cry out, after he had arranged the spectators by beating their shins, "Mind your pockets all round." The name of Vinegar has been frequently given to crabbed ringmakers and boxers. Ward, in his "London Spy," thus introduces a Vinegar champion:

> "Bred up i' th' fields of Lincoln's Inn,
>   Where *Vinegar* reigns master;
> The forward youth doth thence begin
> A broken head to loose or win,
>   For shouts, or for a plaister."

It is to be hoped that this industrious man has saved some little to support him when his sinews are unable to do their duty; for it would be extremely hard, that a man who has conducted himself with such honesty, punctuality, and rigid perseverance, should be dependent on the parish, particularly as he declares, and Conway may be believed, that he never got drunk in his life. The present writer was much obliged to this man for a deliverance from a mob. He had when at Bow commenced a drawing of a Lascar, and before he had completed it, he found himself surrounded by several of their leaders, who were much enraged, conceiving that he was taking a description of the man's person in order to complain of him. Conway happened to come up at the moment, and immediately exclaimed, "Dear heart, no, this gentleman took my picture off the other day, he only does it for his amusement; I know where he lives; he don't want to hurt the man;" on hearing which speech, a publican kindly took upon him to appease the Lascars.

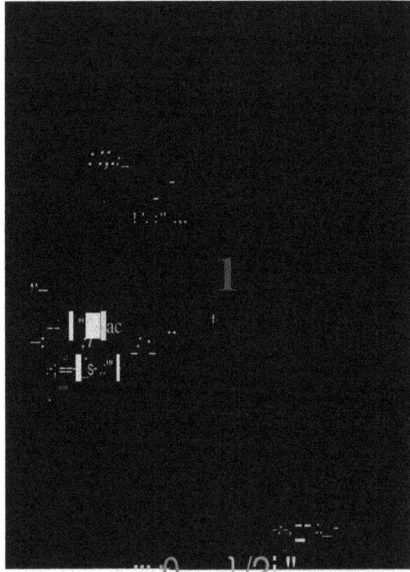

DANCING DOLLS.

PLATE XXI.

B Y all the aged persons with whom the author has conversed, it is agreed that from the time of Hogarth to the present day the street strollers with their Dancing Dolls on a board have not appeared.

The above artist, whose eye glanced at every description of nature, and whose mind was perpetually alive to those scenes which would in any way illustrate his various subjects, has introduced, in his inimitable print of Southwark Fair, the figure of a little man, at that time extremely well known in London, who performed various tricks with two dancing dolls strung to a flat board; his music was the bagpipes, on which he played quick or slow tunes, according to the expression he wished to give his puppets. These dolls were fastened to a board, and moved by a string attached to his knee, as appears in the figure of the boy represented in the present Plate. Since the late Peace, London has been infested with ten or twelve of these lads, natives of Lucca, whose importunities were at first made with all their native impudence and effrontery, for they attempted to thrash the English boys that stood between their puppets and the spectators, but in this they so frequently were mistaken that they behave now with a little more propriety.

The sounds they produce from their drums during the action of their dolls are full of noise and discord, nor are they masters of three notes of their flute. Lucca is also the birth place of most of those people who visit England to play the street organ, carry images, or attend dancing bears or dolls. In Italy there are many places which retain their peculiar trades and occupations; as for example, one village is inhabited by none but shoemakers, whose ancestors resided in the same place and followed a similar employment.

SPRIG OF SHILLELAH AND SHAMROCK SO GREEN.

PLATE XXII.

THE annexed etching was taken from Thomas M'Conwick, an Irishman, who traverses the western streets of London, as a vendor of matches, and, like most of his good-tempered countrymen, has his joke or repartee at almost every question put to him, duly attempered with native wit and humour. M'Conwick sings many of the old Irish songs with excellent effect, but more particularly that of the "Sprig of Shillelah and Shamrock so green," dances to the tunes, and seldom fails of affording amusement to a crowded auditory.

The throne at St. James's was first used on the Birth Day of Queen Charlotte, after the union of the Kingdoms of Great Britain and Ireland, and the Shamrock, the badge of the Irish nation, is introduced among the decorations upon it.

M'Conwick assured me, when he came to London, that the English populace were taken with novelty, and that by either moving his feet, snapping his fingers, or passing a joke upon some one of the surrounding crowd, he was sure of gaining money. He carries matches as an article of sale, and thereby does not come under the denomination of a pauper. Now and then, to please his benefactors, he will sport a bull or two, and when the laugh is increasing a little too much against him, will, in a low tone, remind them that bulls are not confined to the lower orders of Irish. The truth of this assertion may be seen in Miss Edgworth's Essay on Irish bulls, published 1803, from which the following is an extract:

"When Sir Richard Steele was asked how it happened that his countrymen made so many bulls, he replied, 'It is the effect of climate, sir; if an Englishman were born in Ireland, he would make as many.'" However, great mistakes are sometimes made by the wisest of the English; for it is reported of Sir Isaac Newton, that after he had caused a great hole to be made in his study door for his cat to creep through, he had a small one for the kitten.

When the present writer gave this Irishman a shilling for standing for his portrait, he exclaimed, "Thanks to your honour, an acre of performance is worth the whole land of promise."

GINGERBREAD NUTS, OR JACK'S LAST SHIFT.

PLATE XXIII.

THE etching in front of the present Plate, was taken from Daniel Clarey, an industrious Irishman, well known to the London schoolboy as a gingerbread-nut lottery office keeper. Dan had fought for his country as a seaman, and though from some unlucky circumstance he is not entitled to the comforts of Greenwich Hospital, still he boasts of the honour of losing his leg in an engagement on the "Salt Seas." Rendered almost destitute by the loss of his limb, he was nevertheless not wanting in wit to gain a livelihood, and became a vendor of gingerbread-nuts, which he disposed of by way of lottery, and humourously calls this employment, "Jack's last Shift." Though Dan is inferior in some respects to his lively countryman McConwick, who has afforded theme for the preceding pages, yet he is blessed with a sufficient memory to recollect what he has heard, and has persuasive eloquence enough to assure the boys that his lottery is no "South Sea Bubble," where, as he tells them, "not even saw-dust was produced, when deal boards were promised; but that every adventurer in his scheme is sure of having a prize from seven to one hundred nuts, there being no blanks to damp the courage of any enterprizing youth; that some of his gingerbread shot are so highly seasoned that they are as hot as the noble Nelson's balls when he last peppered the jackets of England's foes." The manner of obtaining these gingerbread prizes is as follows:—The hollow box held by Clarey has twenty-seven holes variously numbered, and any one of the strings at the bottom of the box being pulled, causes a doll's head to appear at the hole, which decides, according to its number, the good or ill fortune of the halfpenny adventurer. He acknowledges to his surrounding visitors that he "knows nothing of the lingo of his predecessors, the famed Tiddy Dolls of their day, but that he is quite certain that if *their* gingerbread rolled down the throat like a wheel-barrow, *his* nuts are far superior, for that, should any one of his noble friends prove so fortunate as to draw a prize of one hundred of them, he would be entitled to those of half the usual size, so delicately small that they would be no bigger than the quack doctor's pills, who chalks his name on the walls far and near about London; and as for the innocency of these little pills, he had been assured by a leading member of the Society for the Suppression of Vice, who was very fond of tasting them, that they would do no harm to an *infant babe*, no, not even if they were given it on a Sunday within church time." This mode of gulling the boys with nuts of half the size, if they won a double prize, was equalled by a well-known churchwarden, within these few years, who, upon his coming into office, ordered threepenny loaves to be made instead of sixpenny, so that he might be respectfully saluted by as many more poor people as he passed through the church-yard on a Sunday after his distribution, and thereby obtain popularity. Nor is the device in question very dissimilar to the mode adopted in some modern private lotteries, where there are no blanks to chagrin the purchasers.

The simpleton who attempts to sell gingerbread-nuts gains but little custom compared with the man of dashing wit; and there have been many of the latter description on the town within memory, particularly, about thirty-five years ago, a short red-nosed fellow in a black bushy wig, who trundled a wheel-barrow through St. Martin's Court, Cranbourn Alley, and the adjacent passages. This man, who was attended by a drab of a wife to take the money, was master of much drollery; he would contrast the heated polities of the day with the mildness of his gingerbread, to the no small amusement of Mr. Sheridan, who, when on his way to the election meetings held at the Shakspeare tavern, in favour of his friend Mr. Fox, was once seen to smile and pouch this fellow a shilling; that distinguished mark of approbation from the author of the "School for Scandal" being gained by this gingerbread man by means of the following couplet:

> "May Curtis, with his "Speedy Peace, and soon,"
> Send gingerbread up to the man in the moon."

This fellow would frequently boast of his having danced Horne Tooke upon his knee when he was shopman to that gentleman's father, then a poulterer, or, in genteeler terms, a "Turkey Merchant," called by the vulgar a "Feather Butcher," at the time he lived in Newport Market.

This humourist had his pensioners like the dog and cat's meat man, nor would he ever pass any of them without distributing his broken gingerbread and bits of biscuit: he was particularly kind to one man, who may yet be within the recollection of many persons; he was short in stature carried a wallet, and wore a red cap, and would begin his walk through May's Buildings at six in the evening and arrive safely by nine at Bedford Bury. In his progress he would repeat the song of "Taffy was a Welchman," upon an average, eight times within an hour; and, in order that his singing might be of a piece with his crawling movements, his lengthened tones were made to pass through his nose in so inarticulate a manner as frequently to induce boys to shake him from a supposed slumber. His name was Richard Richards, but from his extreme sloth he was nicknamed by his broken-biscuit benefactor "Mr. Step-an-hour." The money made by the gingerbread heroes is hardly credible;

however, it is of little use, as the profits are generally spent in gin and hot suppers.

CHICKWEED AND GROUNDSEL.

PLATE XXIV.

THE subject of this Plate is George Smith, a Brush-maker out of employ, in consequence of frequent visitations of the rheumatism. This man, finding affliction increase upon him in so great a degree as to render him incapable of pursuing his usual occupation, determined on selling chickweed, an article easily procured without money, and for which there is a certainty of meeting at least one customer in almost every street, as there are scarcely three houses together without their singing birds.

After a very short trial of his new calling, he found he had no occasion to cry his chickweed, for that if he only stood with it before the house, so that the birds could see it, the noise they made was sufficient, as they generally attracted the notice of some one of the family, who soon perceived that the little songsters were chirping at the chickweed man. This can readily be believed by all those who keep birds, for the breaking of a single seed will elate them.

Bryant, in his "Flora Diætetica," p. 94, speaking of the article in question, says, "This is a small annual plant, and a very troublesome weed in gardens. The stalks are weak, green, hairy, succulent, branched, about eight inches long, and lodge on the ground. The leaves are numerous, nearly oval, sharp-pointed, juicy, of the colour of the stalks, and stand on longish footstalks, having membranous bases, which are furnished with long hairs at their edges. The flowers are produced at the bosoms of the leaves, on long slender pedicles; they are small and white, consist of five split petals each, and contain five stamina and three styles. The leaves of this plant have much the flavour of corn-sallad, and are eaten in the same manner. They are deemed refrigorating and nutritive, and excellent for those of a consumptive habit of body. The plant formerly stood recommended in the shops as a vulnerary."

Buchan says of groundsel, "This weed grows commonly in gardens, fields, and upon walls, and bears small yellow flowers and downy seeds; it does not often grow above eight inches high: the stalk is round, fleshy, tolerably straight, and green or reddish; the leaves are oblong, remarkably broad at the bases, blunt, and deeply indented at the edges; the flowers grow in a kind of long cups, at the top of the stalks and branches. It flowers through all the milder months of the year. The juice of this herb, taken in ale, is esteemed a gentle and very good emetic, bringing on vomiting without any great irritation or pain. It assists pains in the stomach, evacuates phlegm, cures the jaundice, and destroys worms. Applied externally, it is said to cleanse the skin of foul eruptions."

BILBERRIES.

PLATE XXV.

BILBERRIES are a modern article of sale, and were first brought to London about forty years ago by countrymen, who appeared in their smock-frocks, with every character of rusticity. In the course of a little time, bilberries were so eagerly bought that it induced many persons to become vendors, and they are now brought to the markets as a regular article of consumption for the season.

These berries mostly grow in Hertfordshire, from whence indeed they are brought to town in very high perfection, and are esteemed by the housewife as wholesome food when made into a pudding; and, though usually sold at fourpence a pint, they are sometimes admitted to the genteel table in a tart.

Dr. Buchan has the following remarks on the Bilberry-bush: he says that it is "a little tough shrubby plant, common in our boggy woods, and upon wet heaths. The stalks are tough, angular, and green; the leaves are small; they stand singly, not in pairs, and are broad, short, and indented about the edges. The flowers are small but pretty, their colour is a faint red, and they are hollow like a cup. The berries are as large as the biggest pea; they are of a blackish colour, and of a pleasant taste. A syrup made of the juice of bilberries, when not over ripe, is cooling and binding."

Among the former Cries of London, those of Elderberries, Dandelion, &c. were not unfrequent, and each had in its turn physicians as well as village doctresses to recommend them. "The inner part of the Elderberry-tree," says Dr. Buchan, "is reputed to cure dropsies, when taken in time, frequently repeated and long persevered in; a cooling ointment is made by boiling the flowers in lard till they are crisp, and then straining it off; the juice of the berries boiled down with sugar, or without, till it comes to the consistence of honey, is the celebrated rob of elder, highly extolled in colds and sore throats, though of late years it seems to have yielded to the preparations of black currants. Wine is made from elderberries, which somewhat resembles Frontiniac in flavour."

The same author says of Dandelion, that "the root is long, large, and white within; every part of the plant is full of milky juice, but most of all the root, from which, when it is broken, it flows plentifully, and is bitterish, but not disagreeable to the taste."

The leaves are sometimes eaten as sallad when very young, and in some parts of the Continent they are blanched like celery for this purpose; taken this way, in sufficient quantity, they are a remedy for the scurvy.

Bryant, in his "Flora Diætetica," page 103, says, "The young tender leaves are eaten in the spring as lettuce, they being much of the same nature, except that they are rather more detergent and diuretic. Boerhaave greatly recommended the use of dandelion in most chronical distempers, and held it capable of resolving all kinds of coagulations, and most obstinate obstructions of the viscera, if it were duly continued. For these purposes the stalks may be blanched and eaten as celery."

There is a fashion in the Cries of London as there are "tides in the affairs of men," particularly in articles that are used as purifiers of the blood. About fifty years ago, nothing but Scurvy-grass was thought of, and the best scurvy-grass ale was sold in Covent Garden, at the public-house at the corner of Henrietta Street.

SIMPLERS.

Plate XXVI.

THOSE persons who live in the country and rise with the sun can bear testimony to the activity of the Simpler, who commences his selections from the ditches and swampy grounds at that early period of the day, and, after he has filled a large pack for his back, trudges for fifteen miles to the London markets, where perhaps he is the first who offers goods for sale; he then returns back and sleeps in some barn until the next succeeding sun. Such an instance of rustic simplicity is William Friday, whose portrait is exhibited in the annexed plate. This man starts from Croydon, with champignons, mushrooms, &c. and is alternately snail-picker, leech-bather, and viper-catcher. Simpling is not confined to men; but women, particularly in some counties, often constitute a greater part of the community, and they appear to be a distinct class of beings. The plate which accompanies this description exhibits three women Simplers returning from market to Croydon; they were sketched on the Stockwell Road, and are sufficient to shew their gait.

The Simplers, particularly the women, are much attached to brass rings, which they display in great profusion upon almost every finger: their faces and arms are sunburnt and freckled, and they live to a great age, notwithstanding their constant wet and heavy burthens, which are always earned on the loins.

To the exertions of these poor people the public are much indebted, as they supply our wants every day; indeed the extensive sale of their commodities, which they dispose of to the herb-shops in Covent Garden, Fleet, and Newgate Markets, must at once declare them to be a most useful set of people. Among the numerous articles culled from the hedges and the springs, the following are a few in constant consumption: water-cresses, dandelions, scurvy-grass, nettles, bitter-sweet, cough-grass, feverfew, hedge mustard, Jack by the hedge, or sauce-alone.

Dr. Buchan observes, that "Bitter-sweet is a common wild plant, with weak but woody stalks, that runs among our hedges, and bears bunches of pretty blue flowers in summer, and in autumn red berries; the stalks run to ten feet in length, but they cannot support themselves upright; they are of a bluish colour, and, when broken, have a very disagreeable smell like rotten eggs. The leaves are oval, but sharp-pointed, and have each two little ones near the base; they are of a dusky green and indented, and they grow singly on the

78

stalks. The flowers are small and of a fine purplish blue, with yellow threads in the middle; the berries are oblong."

The same author, speaking of Cough-grass, says, "However offensive this weed may be in the fields and gardens, it is said to have its uses in medicine, and should teach us that the most common things are not therefore despicable, since it is certain that nothing was made in vain."

The Doctor observes, that "Jack by the hedge, or sauce alone, is an annual plant, which perishes every year, but makes a figure in the spring, and is common in our hedges. The root is small, white, and woody, the stalks rise to the height of three feet, and are slender, channelled, hairy, and very straight. The leaves, which stand on long foot-stalks, are large, broad, short, and roundish; and those which grow on the stalk somewhat pointed at the extremities, and waved at the edges. They are of a pale yellow green colour, thin and slender, and being bruised, smell like onions or garlic. The flowers, which stand ten or a dozen together at the tops of the branches, are small and white, consisting each of four leaves; these are followed by slender pods, containing small longish seeds. It is found in hedges, and on bank sides, and flowers in May."

Many of the simples of England are peculiar to particular spots, as the following extract from Gerarde's Herbal, fol. 1633, Lond. edited by Thomas Johnson, will demonstrate. "Navelwort, or wall penniwoort. The first kind of penniwoort groweth plentifully in Northampton upon every stone wall about the towne, at Bristow, Bathe, Wells, and most places of the West Countrie, upon stone walls. It groweth upon Westminster Abbey, over the doore that leadeth from Chaucer's tombe to the old palace." From an address to his courteous readers, it appears that Gerarde first established his Herbal in the year 1597, in the month of December, and that he then resided in Holborn. Thomas Johnson, Gerarde's editor, dates his address to his reader from his house on Snow Hill, Oct. 22, 1633. Hence it will appear that any thing these writers may have said respecting the structure of the buildings or topography of the suburbs in which they herbarized, is to be depended upon.

Snails are brought to market by the Simpler, and continue to be much used by consumptive persons. There are various sorts which are peculiar to particular spots; for instance, at Gayhurst, in Buckinghamshire, the Helix Pomœria were there turned down for the use of Lady Venetia Digby when in a weak state. The house now belongs to Miss Wright, a descendant of Lord Keeper Wright, where these snails continue in great profusion. Near the old green-houses built by Kent in Kensington Gardens, the same snail is frequently found; it has a yellow shell, and was prescribed and placed there for William the Third.

Vipers formerly were sold in quantities at the Simpling Shops, but of late years they are so little called for that not above one in a month is sold in Covent Garden Market. There were regular viper catchers, who had a method of alluring them with a bit of scarlet cloth tied to the end of a long stick.

The following lines are extracted from a curious half-sheet print, entitled, "The Cries of London," to the tune of "Hark, the merry merry Christ Church bells," printed and sold at the printing office in Bow Church Yard, London. To this plate are prefixed two very curious old wood-blocks, one of a Galantie-show man, of the time of King William the Third, and the other of the time of James the First, representing a Salt-box man, and is perhaps one of the earliest specimens of that character. The lines alluded to are:

> "Here's fine rosemary, sage, and thyme!
> Come buy my ground ivy.
> Here's fetherfew, gilliflowers, and rue,
> Come buy my knotted marjorum, ho!
> Come buy my mint, my fine green mint,
> Here's fine lavender for your clothes,
> Here's parsley and winter-savory,
> And hearts-ease, which all do choose.
> Here's balm and hissop, and cinquefoil,
> All fine herbs, it is well known.
> > Let none despise the merry merry Cries
> > Of famous London Town!
>
> Here's pennyroyal and marygolds!
> Come buy my nettle-tops.
> Here's water-cresses and scurvy-grass!
> Come buy my sage of virtue ho!
> Come buy my wormwood and mugwort,
> Here's all fine herbs of every sort.
> Here's southernwood that's very good,
> Dandelion and houseleek.
> Here's dragon's tongue and wood sorrel,
> With bear's foot and horehound.
> > Let none despise the merry merry Cries
> > Of famous London Town!"

WASHER-WOMEN, CHAR-WOMEN, AND STREET NURSES.

Plate XXVII.

Perhaps there is not a class of people who work harder than those washer-women who go out to assist servants in what is called a heavy wash; they may be seen in the winter time, shivering at the doors, at three and four o'clock in the morning, and are seldom dismissed before ten at night, this hard treatment being endured for two shillings and sixpence a day. They may be divided into two classes, the industrious, who labour cheerfully to support their little ones, and, too often, an idle and cruel husband; and those that take snuff, drink gin, and propagate the scandal of the neighbourhood, seldom quitting the house of their employer without gaining the secrets of the family, which they acquire by pretending to tell the fortunes of every one in the house to the servants of the family, by the manner in which the grouts of the tea adhere to the sides of the tea-cup. Most of these people, who are generally round-shouldered and lop-sided, are so accustomed to chatter with the servants, that they acquire a habit of keeping their mouths open, either horizontally or perpendicularly; and it is evident from Hollar's etchings of Leonardo da Vinci's caricatures that the latter must have studied the grimaces of this class of people. Some of these old washer-women, when they happen to meet with a discreet and silent domestic, will speak to the cat or the dog, and even hold conversation with themselves rather than lose the privilege of utterance.

These wretches are always full of complaints of their coughs, asthmas, or pains in the stomach, but these are mere efforts to procure an extra glass of cordial.

The Char-women are that description of people who go about to clean houses, either by washing the wainscot, scrubbing the floors, or brightening the pots and kettles; they are generally worse drabs, if possible, than the lowest order of washer-women; they will either filch the soap, steal the coals, or borrow a plate, which they never return; and yet the women of this calling who conduct themselves with sobriety and honesty, are great acquisitions to single gentlemen, particularly students in the law.

Few families, however watchful they may be over the conduct of their servants, are aware of the extreme idleness and profligacy of some of them.

If the mistress of a house would for once rise at five o'clock, she might behold a set of squalid beings engaged in whitening the steps of the doors; she may even observe some of them, who have procured keys of the area gates, descend the steps to procure from the kitchen pails of hog-wash, with meat and bread wrapped up in tattered aprons; so that their servants, by thus getting rid of the door-cleaning business, remain in bed after the milkwoman, by the help of a string, has lowered her can into the area. This dishonesty of the servants has been extended, from a few broken crusts, to the more generous gift of half a loaf in a morning.

On the contrary, it is a fact too well known, that there are many servants who rise too early, particularly those who attend to the flattery of men who sneak into houses, pretending to be in love with their charming persons, merely for the purpose of obtaining the surest mode of robbing the house, either then or in future.

There are hundreds of old women who take charge of the children of those who go out for daily hire. These Nurses drag the infants in all sorts of ways about the streets for the whole day, and sometimes treat them very ill, and, imitating the mode usually adopted by the vulgar part of nurses in families, to pacify the squalling and too often hungry infants, terrify them with a threat that Tom Poker, David Stumps, or Bonaparte, are coming to take them away. This custom of frightening children, which was practised in very early times, was made use of by the Spanish nurses after the defeat of the Armada. Burton, in his "Anatomy of Melancholy," part I, sec. 2: "Education a cause of Melancholy. There is a great moderation to be had in such things as matters of so great moment, to the making or marring of a childe. Some fright their children with beggars, bugbears, and hobgoblins, if they cry or be otherways unruly."

Among the very few single prints published in the reign of Queen Elizabeth, there is one engraved on wood, measuring twenty inches by thirteen; it contains multitudes of figures, and is so great a rarity, that the author has seen only one impression of it, which is in the truly valuable and interesting collection of prints presented in the most liberal manner to the British Museum by Sir Joseph and Lady Banks.

This print, which has escaped the notice of all the writers on the Graphic Art, is entitled, "Tittle-Tattle, or the several Branches of Gossipping;" at the foot of the print are the following verses, evidently in a type and orthography of a later time:

1.
At childbed when the gossips meet,
Fine stories we are told;

83

And if they get a cup too much,
    Their tongues they cannot hold.

2.

At market when good housewives meet,
    Their market being done,
Together they will crack a pot
    Before they can get home.

3.

The bakehouse is a place, you know,
    Where maids a story hold,
And if their mistresses will prate,
    They must not be controll'd.

4.

At alehouse you see how jovial they be,
    With every one her noggin;
For till the skull and belly be full
    None of them will be jogging.

5.

To Church fine ladies do resort,
    New fashions for to spy,
And others go to Church sometimes,
    To shew their bravery.

6.

Hot-house makes a rough skin smooth,
    And doth it beautify;
Fine gossips use it every week,
    Their skins to purify.

7.

At the conduit striving for their turn,
    The quarrel it grows great,
That up in arms they are at last,
    And one another beat.

8.

Washing at the river's side
    Good housewives take delight;

But scolding sluts care not to work,
    Like wrangling queens they fight.

9.

Then gossips all a warning take,
    Pray cease your tongue to rattle;
Go knit, and sew, and brew, and bake,
    And leave off TITTLE-TATTLE.

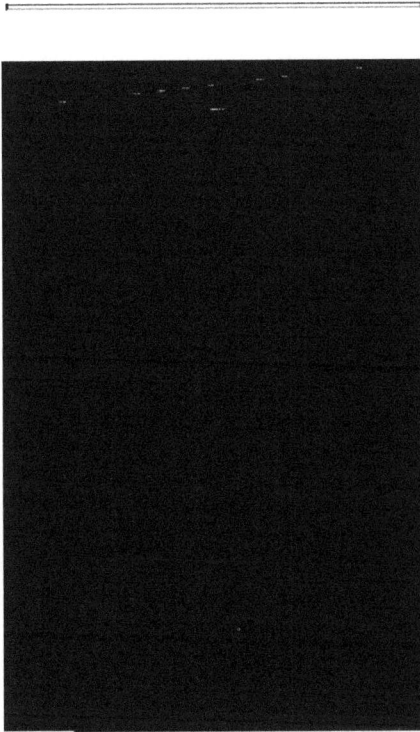

SMITHFIELD SALOOP.

PLATE XXVIII.

ABOUT a century ago, almost every corner of the more public streets was occupied at midnight, until six or seven in the morning, by the sellers of frumenty, barley broth, cow-heel soup, and baked ox-cheek; and in those days when several hundreds of chairmen were nightly waiting in the metropolis, and it was the fashion for the bloods of the day to beat the rounds, as they termed it, there was a much greater consumption of such refreshments.

The scenes of vice at the above period were certainly far more frequent than they are at present, for hard drinking, and the visitation of brothels were then esteemed as the completion of what was termed genteel education; and it was no unusual thing to see the famous Quin, with his inseparable associate Frank Hayman, the painter, swearing at each other in the kennel, but both with a full determination to remain there until the watchman went his round.

The numerous songs of the day, and the incomparable plates by Hogarth, will sufficiently show the folly and vice of those drinking times, when the courtier, after attending the drawing-room of St. James's, would walk in his full dress, with bag and sword, from the palace, to the diabolical coffee-room of Moll King, in Covent Garden, where he would mix, sit, and converse with every description of character.

Moll King's was the house now the sign of the Green Man, and was a mere hovel, so destitute of accommodation that the principal chamber of vice was immediately over the coffee room, and could only be ascended by a drop ladder.

Saloop, the subject of this etching, has superseded almost every other midnight street refreshment, being a beverage easily made, and a long time considered as a sovereign cure for head-ache arising from drunkenness. But no person, unless he has walked through the streets from the hour of twelve, can duly paint the scenes of the saloop stall with its variety of customers.

Whoever may be desirous of tasting saloop in the highest perfection, may be gratified at Reid's Coffee House,[16] No. 102, Fleet Street, which was the first respectable house where it was to be had, and established in the year 1719. The following lines are painted on a board, and suspended in the coffee room:

> "Come all degrees now passing by,
> My charming liquor taste and try;

86

To Lockyer[17] come, and drink your fill;
Mount Pleasant[18] has no kind of ill.
The fumes of wine, punch, drams, and beer,
It will expell; your spirits cheer;
From drowsiness your spirits free.
Sweet as a rose your breath shall be.
Come taste and try, and speak your mind;
Such rare ingredients here are joined,
Mount Pleasant pleases all mankind."

The following extract respecting saloop, is taken from p. 38 of "Flora Diætetica, or History of Esculent Plants," by Charles Bryant, of Norwich, 1783. "Orchis Mascula. This is very common in our woods, meadows, and pastures, and the powdered roots of it are said to be the saloop which is sold in the shops; but the shop roots come from Turkey.

"The flowers of most of the plants of this genus are indiscriminately called cuckoo-flowers by the country people. Though it has been affirmed that saloop is the root of the mascula only, yet those of the morio, and of some other species of orchis, will do equally as well, as I can affirm from my own experience; consequently, to give a description of the mascula in particular will be useless. As most country people are acquainted with these plants by the name of cuckoo-flowers, it certainly would be worth their while to employ their children to collect the roots for sale; and though they may not be quite so large as those that come from abroad, yet they may be equally as good, and as they are exceedingly plentiful, enough might annually be gathered for our own consumption, and thus a new article of employment would be added to the poorer sort of people.

"The time for taking them up is when the seed is about ripe, as then the new bulbs are fully grown; and all the trouble of preparing them is, to put them, fresh taken up, into scalding hot water for about half a minute; and on taking them out, to rub off the outer skin; which done, they must be laid on tin plates, and set in a pretty fierce oven for eight or ten minutes, according to the size of the roots; after this, they should be removed to the top of the oven, and left there till they are dry enough to pound.

"Saloop is a celebrated restorative among the Turks, and with us it stands recommended in consumptions, bilious cholics, and all disorders proceeding from an acrimony in the juices.

"Some people have a method of candying the roots, and thus prepared they are very pleasant, and may be eaten with good success against coughs and inward soreness."

SMITHFIELD PUDDING.

Plate XXIX.

IT would be almost criminal to proceed in my account of the present cry without passing a due encomium on the subject of it. The good qualities of an English pudding, more especially when it happens to be enriched with the due portion of enticing plums, are well known to most of us. It is a luxury to which our Gallic neighbours are entire strangers, and an article of cookery worth any dozen of their harlequin kick-shaws.

The justly-celebrated comedian, Ned Shuter, was so passionately fond of this article that he would never dine without it, and anything that led to the bare mention of a pudding would burst the silence of a couple of hours' smoking; he was on one occasion known to lay down his pipe, and to exclaim, that the dinner the gentleman had just described would have been a very good one if there had but been a plum-pudding. The places where this excellent commodity is chiefly exposed to sale in the manner described in the engraving, are those of the greatest traffic or publicity, such as Smithfield on a market morning, where waggoners, butchers, and drovers, are sure to find their pence for a slice of hot pudding. Fleet Market, Leadenhall, Honey Lane, and Spital Fields, have each their hot-pudding men. In the lowest neighbourhoods in Westminster, where the soldiers reside, cook-shops find great custom for their pudding. The stalls, near the Horse Guards always have large quantities ready cut into penny slices, piled up like boards in a timber-yard.

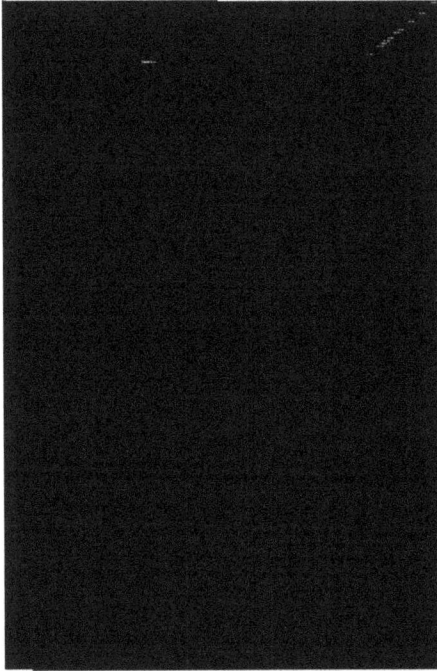

At the time of relieving guard, vendors of pudding are always to be found on the parade. There is a black man, a handsome, well-made fellow, remarkably clean in his person, and always drest in the neatest manner, who never fails to sell his pudding; he also frequents the Regent's Park on a Sunday afternoon, and, though he has no wit, his nonsense pleases the crowd. This person, who is now at the top of his calling, had a predecessor of the name of Eglington, who likewise carried on the business of a tailor.

He was a well-made and very active man, and by reason of his being seen in various parts of London nearly at the same time, was denominated the "Flying Pudding Man." His principal walk was in the neighbourhood of Fleet Market and Holborn Bridge, and his smartness of dress and quickness of repartee gained the attention of his customers; he seldom appeared but in a state of perfect sobriety, and many curious anecdotes are related of him.

On the approach of Edmonton Fair, wishing to see the sports and pastimes of the place, he ordered his wife to make as many puddings as to fill a hackney coach. This being done, on the morning of the opening of the fair a coach was hired for the puddings, and the pudding man and pudding lady took their seats by the side of the coachman. On their arrival at the fair he put on his well-known dress, and instantly commenced his cry of "pudding," whilst the lady supplied him from the coach. In a few hours' time, when his stock was all disposed of, he resumed his best attire, and with his fair spouse proceeded to visit the various shows.

His well-known features were soon recognized by thousands who frequented the fair, and their jeers of "hot, hot, smoking hot," resounded from booth to booth. At the close of the day this constant couple walked home well laden with the profits they had made. There is hardly a fight on the Scrubs,[19] nor a walking match on Blackheath, that are not visited by the pudding men.

When malefactors were executed at Tyburn, the pudding men of the day were sure to be there, and indeed so many articles were sold, and the cries of new milk, curds and whey, spice cakes, barley sugar, and hot spice gingerbread, were so numerous and loud, that this place on the day of execution was usually designated by the thousands of blackguards who attended it under the appellation of Tyburn Fair. The reader may see a faithful representation of this melancholy and humourous scene by the inimitable Hogarth, in the Execution Plate of his Idle Apprentice. In this engraving he will also find a correct figure of the triangular gallows, commonly called the "Three-legged Mare," and which stood upon the site afterwards occupied by the turnpike house, at the end of Oxford Street.

In many instances the pudding sold in the streets has a favourable aspect, and under some circumstances perhaps proves a delicious treat to the purchaser.

Nothing can be more gratifying than to enable a poor little chimney-sweeper to indulge his appetite with a luxury before which he has for some minutes been standing with a longing inclination; and as this gratification can be accomplished at a very trifling expense, it were surely much better to behold it realized than to see the canting Tabernacle beggar carry away the pennies he has obtained to the gin shop. It gives the writer great pleasure to state to the readers of Jonas Hanway's little tract in defence of chimney-sweepers, that, after witnessing with the most painful sensations the great and wanton cruelty which has for years been exercised upon that defenceless object the infant chimney-sweeper, he has of late frequently visited several houses of their masters, where he found in some instances that they had much better treatment than formerly, and, to the credit of many of the masters, that the boys had been as well taken care of, as to bedding and food, as the nature of their wretched calling could possibly admit of. By three or four of the principal master chimney-sweepers, the boys were regaled on Sundays with the old English fare of roast beef and plum pudding. Whatever may be the opinion of grave and elderly persons with respect to the lads of the present day, who as soon as they are indulged with a dandy coat by their silly mothers strut about like jackdaws and attempt to look big, even upon their grandfathers, yet we must declare, and perhaps to the satisfaction of these little men of sixteen, that they do not stand alone, for even some of the chimney-sweepers' boys, particularly those of the higher masters, regard the custom of dancing about the streets on May-day as low and vulgar, and prefer visiting the tea gardens, where they can display their shirt collars drawn up to their eyes.

Certain it is that the greater number of those who now perambulate the streets as chimney-sweeps on May-day, are in reality disguised gypsies, cinder-sifters, and nightmen. Nor is the protraction of this ceremony in modern times from one to three days, even by its legitimate owners, unworthy of notice in this place; inasmuch as there is good reason for supposing that the money collected during the first two of those days is transferred to the pockets of the masters, instead of being applied for the benefit of the poor boys, whilst the well-meant benevolence of the public is shamefully deluded.

THE BLADDER MAN.

PLATE XXX.

WITHIN the memory of the author's oldest friends, London has been visited by men similar to Bernardo Millano, whose figure is pourtrayed in the following Plate. About sixty years ago there was a Turk, of a most pompous appearance, who entertained crowds in the street by playing on an instrument of five strings passed over a bladder, and drawn up to the ends of a long stick, something like that exhibited in the etching, and which instrument is said to have been the original hurdy-gurdy. This Turk contrived by the assistance of his nose, which was a pretty large one, to produce a noise with which most of the spectators seemed to be pleased. The splendour of his dress, and the pomposity of his manner, procured him a livelihood for some years. His success induced other persons to imitate him; the most remarkable of whom was the famous Matthew Skeggs, who actually played a concerto on a broomstick, at the Little Theatre in the Haymarket, in the character of Signor Bumbasto. His portrait was painted by Thomas King, a particular friend of Hogarth, and engraved by Houston. Skeggs, who then kept a public-house, the sign of the "Hoop and Bunch of Grapes," in St. Alban's Street, now a part of Waterloo Place, published it himself. Skeggs's celebrity is noticed in the following extract from G. A. Stevens: "The choice spirits have ever been famous for their talents as musical artists. They usually met at the harvest-homes of grape gathering. There, exhilarated by the pressings of the vintage, they were wont to sing songs, tell stories, and show tricks, from their first emerging until their perihelion under the presidentship of Mr. George Alexander Stevens, Ballad-Laureat to the Society of Choice Spirits, and who appeared at Ranelagh in the character of Comus, supported by those drolls of merry memory. Unparalleled were their performances, as *first fists* upon the salt-box, and inimitable the variations they would twang upon the *forte* and *piano* Jew's harp; excellent was *Howard* in the chin concerto, whose nose also supplied the unrivalled tones of the bagpipe. Upon the sticcado, *Matt. Skeggs* remains still unrivalled. And we cannot now boast of one real genius upon the genuine hurdy-gurdy. Alas! these stars are all extinguished; and the remains of ancient British harmony are now confined to the manly music of the marrow-bones and cleavers. Everything must sink into oblivion. Corn now grows where Troy town stood; Ranelagh may be metamorphosed into a methodists' meeting-house; Vaux-Hall cut into skittle alleys; the two Theatres converted into auction rooms; and the New Pantheon become the stately

habitation of some Jew pawnbroker: nay, the Sons of Liberty themselves,
&c."

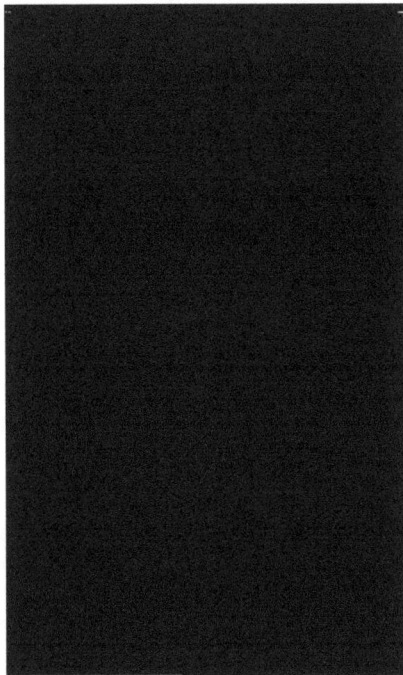

Much about this time another Bladder-man was in high estimation, whose
portrait has been handed down to us in an etching by Miller, from a most
spirited drawing by Gravelot. The following verses, which set forth his woful
situation, are placed at the foot of the Plate:

1.

"No musick ever charm'd my mind
So much as bladder fill'd with wind;
But as no mortal's free from fate,
Nor nothing keeps its first estate,
A pamper'd prodigal unkind
One day with sword let out the wind!
My bladder ceas'd its pleasing sound,
While boys stood tantalizing round.

"They well may laugh who always win,
But, had I not then thought on tin,
My misery had been compleat;
I must have begg'd about the street:
But none to grief should e'er give way:
This canister, ne'er fill'd with tea!
Can please my audience as well,
And charm their ears with, O Brave Nell."

Some few years since a whimsical fellow attracted public notice by passing strings over the skull of a horse, upon which he played as a fidler. Another man, remarkably tall and thin, made a square violin, upon which he played for several years, particularly within the centre arches of Westminster Bridge.

To the eternal honour of the street-players of former times, it will ever be remembered that the great Purcell condescended to set one of their elegies to music. "Thomas Farmer, in 1684, lived in Martlet Court, in Bow Street, Covent Garden. He was originally one of the London street waits, and his elegy was set to music by Purcell." See Hawkins's History of Music, Vol. V. p. 18.

The Guardian, No. 1, March 12, 1713, notices the famous John Gale. "There was, I remember, some years ago, one John Gale, a fellow that played upon a pipe, and diverted the multitude by dancing in a ring they made about him, whose face became generally known, and the artists employed their skill in delineating his features, because every man was judge of the similitude of them."

A sort of guitar or cittern, and also the fiddle, were used in this country so early as the year 1364, and may be seen upon a brass monumental plate to the memory of Robert Braunche and his two wives, in the choir of St. Margaret's Church at Lynn. The subject alluded to is the representation of a Peacock feast, consisting of a long table with twelve persons, besides musicians and other attendants. Engravings of this very curious monument may be seen in Gough's Sepulchral Monuments, vol. i. p. 115; in Carter's Specimens of Ancient Sculpture, vol. ii. plate 15; and in Cotman's Norfolk Brasses, Pl. III. p. 4.

POSTSCRIPT. BY THE EDITOR.

✳ The interest of the Plates in Mr. Smith's "Antient Topography of London," is much increased by numerous spirited little sketches of remarkable characters well known in the streets of the Metropolis; several of whom would have formed valuable additions, either to his work on the London Beggars, intituled, "Vagabondiana," or the present volume: a few of these shall be here noticed.

1. In the View of the Old Houses in London Wall, p. 63, the man with two baskets is JOHN BRYSON, well known in London, particularly in rainy weather. He had been an opulent fishmonger in Bloomsbury Market, but became, by several losses, so reduced, that he latterly carried nothing except nuts in his basket; but his custom to the last was to cry every sort of fish from the turbot to the perriwinkle, never heeding the calls of those unacquainted with his humour. In the same Plate is WILLIAM CONWAY, whose cry of "Hard metal Spoons to sell or change," was familiar to the inhabitants of London and its environs. This man's portrait is also given by Mr. Smith in the present work, p. 63.

2. In the View of old Houses at the West end of Chancery Lane, p. 48, are several figures drawn from the life. The woman with crutches represents ANNE SIGGS. She was remarkable for her cleanliness, a rare quality for her fraternity. Slander, from whose sting the most amiable persons are not invulnerable, tempted this woman to spread a report of her being the sister of the celebrated tragedian, Mrs. Siddons. From a work of singular character by Mr. James Parry, it appears that she was a daughter of an industrious breeches-maker at Dorking in Surrey. Another back view of this woman occurs in the Plate of Duke Street, Smithfield, in p. 54.

3. The man without legs, in the same print, is SAMUEL HORSEY, well known in Holborn, Fleet Street, and the Strand. In 1816 this man had been a London beggar for thirty-one years. He had a most Herculean trunk, and his weather-beaten ruddy face was the picture of health. Mr. Smith has given a back view of this beggar in "Vagabondiana," p. 37, where are some further anecdotes of him.

4. The dwarf hobbling up Chancery Lane was JEREMIAH DAVIES, a native of Wales. He was frequently shewn at fairs, and supported a miserable existence by performing sleight-of-hand tricks. He was also very strong, and would lift a considerable weight, though not above three feet high.

5. The tall slender figure next to Davies was a Mr. CREUSE, a truly singular

man, who never begged of any one, but would not refuse money when offered. He died in Middlesex Court, Drury Lane, and was attended to the burial ground in that street by friends in two mourning coaches. It is said he left money to a considerable amount behind him.

6. In the View of Houses in Sweedon's Passage, p. 42, is a portrait of JOSEPH CLINCH, a noisy bow-legged ballad-singer, who was particularly famous, about 1795, for his song upon Whittington and his Cat. He likewise sold a coarse old woodcut of the animal, with its history and that of its master printed in the back ground.

7. In the view of Winchester Street, p. 68, the person with the umbrella went under the name of Count VERDION, well known to Book Collectors. This person was a professor of languages; for several years frequented Furnival's Inn Coffee-House; and was a member of a man's benefit society held at the Genoa Arms public house, in Hays's Court, Newport Market. This supposed Count eventually proved to be a female, and died of a cancer on the 16th July 1802, at her lodgings in Charles Street, Hatton Garden, in the 58th year of her age.

8. The short figure, carrying a little box, was sketched from the celebrated corn-cutter, Mr. CORDEROY, who married a lady five feet six inches high.

9. The figure beyond Mr. Corderoy, is that of the respectable Bishop of St. POL DE LEON; of whom a portrait and memoir by Mr. Eardley Wilmot, will be found in the Gentleman's Magazine for 1807.

10. In the view of Leadenhall Street, p. 52, the figure with a wig-box in his hands represents JOSEPH WATKINS, born in 1739 at Richmond, in Yorkshire; by trade a barber, and a man of retentive memory. He frequently shaved Hogarth, whom he knew well, and said he was the last person in London who wore a scarlet roquelaure. He had gathered blackberries on the north side of the road now Oxford Street, and remembered the old triangular gallows at Tyburn, as represented in the Execution Plate of the Idle Apprentice.

11. The next figure is that of a draggle-tailed bawler of dying speeches, horrid murders, elegies, &c.

12. The female in a morning jacket was sketched from the celebrated Mrs. ELIZABETH CARTER, the learned translator of Epictetus. She died Feb. 19, 1806.

13. The clumsy figure in a white coat, holding a goose, was well known about town as a vender of aged poultry.

14. The figure with a cocked hat, was a dealer in old iron, a man well known at auctions of building materials, and was nicknamed by the brokers as OLD RUSTY.

In 1815 Mr. Smith published a separate whole-length portrait of "Henry Dinsdale, nicknamed Sir Harry Dimsdale, mayor of the mock Borough of Garret, aged 38, anno 1800." It forms a good companion to his Vagabondiana. Dinsdale was by trade a muffin-man. There is also a spirited head of Dinsdale by Mr. Smith; and his portrait, in his court dress, is copied into Hone's Every Day Book, vol. II. p. 829, where, by mistake, it is called Sir Jeffrey Dunstan.

P. 9. Hand's Bun-house at Chelsea was pulled down April 18, 1839. See Gentleman's Magazine for May 1839.

In p. 54 the cry of "Young Lambs to Sell" is noticed. It may be added, that in Hone's Table Book, p. 396, is a spirited engraving of William Liston, an old soldier, with one arm and one leg, who, in 1821, carried about "Young Lambs to Sell." The *first* crier of "Young Lambs to Sell," Mr. Hone says, "was a maimed sailor, and with him originated the manufacture."

THE END.

www.ingramcontent.com/pod-product-compliance
Ingram Content Group UK Ltd.
Pitfield, Milton Keynes, MK11 3LW, UK
UKHW011336080126
9998UKWH00017B/183